GHOSTS IN THE OLD ATTIC

Book #6
The Sam Cooper Adventure Series

GHOSTS IN THE OLD ATTIC

Book #6
The Sam Cooper Adventure Series

Max Elliot Anderson

Copyright Notice

Cover Design: Anna O'Brien
Interior Design: Anna O'Brien
Editor: Deb Haggerty
Published in Association with Hartline Literary Agency

PUBLISHED BY: Elk Lake Publishing, Inc., 35 Dogwood Dr., Plymouth, MA 02360

Library Cataloging Data
Names: Anderson, Max Elliot (Max Elliot Anderson)
Ghosts in the Old Attic, Book #6, The Sam Cooper Adventure Series, Max Elliot Anderson

p. 21.59cm × 13.97cm (8.5in × 5.5 in.)
Description: Elk Lake Publishing, Inc. digital eBook edition | Elk Lake Publishing, Inc. POD paperback edition | Elk Lake Publishing, Inc. 2016.
Identifiers: ISBN-13: 978-1-944430-99-3(POD) | 978-0-692325-84-1(ebk.)
Key Words: Adventure, Family, Mansion, Pirates, Buried Treasure, Crooks, Louisiana

DEDICATED TO

MY SOUTHERN BELLE
CLAUDIA LYND

CHAPTER 1

I'm too old to be this scared, twelve-year-old Sam whispered. But that was just before he heard heavy chains in the attic again, slowly dragging across wooden beams. It sounded like they were rattling right above his head. Sam Cooper was powerless to do anything to stop them. He couldn't move a muscle. His eyes widened. His heart began pounding. He knew exactly what was going to happen next.

"Turn that thing off," his friend Tyler whimpered. "It's scaring me to death."

"You say that every time it comes to the best part," Tony said.

"The best part is the *worst* part to me. Now turn it off!"

"But it's just gettin' good," Sam said.

"I'm telling your mom and dad if you don't."

"I *hate* it when you say something like that."

"Well, I hate this movie. It's scary and I don't like it. And besides, there isn't a real house like that anyway. It's all pretend."

"That's what makes it so much fun. You can be scared out of your wits, but you know it's not real." Sam reached for the control with his trembling hand and turned off the movie. He and his friends continued sitting on the couch … too afraid to make a move.

Then something terrible happened.

They heard a noise at the front door, and even though it was only late in the afternoon, the guys sat like three frozen statues. Then Tyler scooted under an oversized pillow and held onto it with both arms ... tight.

A click of the doorknob made everyone blink.

Tyler closed his eyes, but Sam turned his head slowly and looked over toward the door.

The knob began turning ... in slow motion.

Then another click.

And the door ... swung ... open. That's when Sam closed his eyes too.

"We're home, guys!" Sam's mother's cheerful voice called out.

Sam took a deep breath and opened his eyes. And his friends opened theirs.

"We've got some news," Sam's father told them.

"Sorry we're so late," his mother added.

Sam's father looked over to Tony and Tyler. "You guys better head on home for supper this time."

"But we ..." Tyler started to say.

"I know," Sam's mother interrupted, "we were planning on having you eat here tonight, but something came up." She smiled. "I'm sorry. We'll just have to do it some other time."

Sam could still hear Tyler grumbling when the door shut. And he wondered what the news could be. He knew his father had taken time off work and made a couple of unexplained trips recently. But, since he was now in the last few weeks of school, he hadn't paid too much attention to that. Still, he had noticed lots of phone calls where his dad kept the door closed.

"I'm hungry," Sam said. "What's the big surprise?"

"Let's go into the kitchen," his father said. "We can talk about it there."

Sam's mother took out hoagie buns, mustard, potato chips,

and juice while his father cut slices from the ham they had had for dinner the night before.

"I like some surprises," Sam said. "If I guess, do I win something?"

His mother smiled. "You'll never guess."

"Is it a dog?"

His father shook his head.

"A new car?" Sam asked.

"No, son."

Then Sam's eyebrows went up. "Wait a minute. I know what it is."

"What?" his mother asked.

"Is it a new brother or sister?"

She laughed. "That really *would* be big news—and a surprise."

Sam thumped his fingers on the counter. "Well, what is it then?"

As they sat at the table, his father prayed for the food and the family. Then, before he finished, he said the strangest thing. "And help us as we take this next big step." After that, the family began eating.

"Those were all good guesses, but I'm afraid you weren't even close."

"Then what?" Sam asked.

"Well," his mother began, "you remember us telling you about your Aunt Claudia and Uncle Ralph, right?"

"And Scooter and Shelly?" Sam replied.

"Yes."

"What about them?"

"Claudia is my sister. We've never gone to visit them in Louisiana."

"Then we're taking a trip? Great!" Sam said.

"It's more than a trip," his father told him.

Sam stared back and tilted his head to one side.

"The family is going to move there."

"I thought their family already did," Sam said.

"No."

"They didn't?"

"No. I mean *this* family is moving there."

"We are? But why?" Sam asked. "I've got all my friends here now. And we have the best basketball team ever. Why now?"

"We know about all that. Only this is going to be good for the whole family."

"But I like it here." The words nearly got caught in his throat.

"As do we," his father said. "But wait till you hear what we plan to do there."

"What?" Sam asked.

"Your mother and I are going to buy an old house around Baton Rouge and change it into a bed and breakfast so tourists can stay there."

"I thought having breakfast in bed was only for special days … or when you get sick," Sam said. "What's a bed and breakfast anyway?"

"It's like a hotel, only smaller. People get to feel like they're staying in someone's house."

Sam groaned. "Sounds like they *will* be … *ours*."

"We'll have our own rooms and special place in the house … away from all our guests."

Sam kept looking at his father. "How big a house are we talking about?"

"An old Southern mansion."

Sam's face brightened. "I kinda like the sound of that."

"You know," his father began, "you know how much I hate moving the family around all the time. We've never been able to put down roots and stay in one place. Now we can."

"Did something happen to your job, Dad?"

"Not this time."

"But I was hoping to stay here all the way through high

school. I mean, I don't know what I'm gonna tell the rest of the guys."

His father thought for a moment, then nodded. "I know. It'll be a real adjustment for all of us. But think of it this way. From now on, we'll have a place to call home and we'll never ever have to leave it unless we want to."

Sam shook his head. "Do they even play basketball in Louisiana?"

His father smiled back. "Yes, they do."

"How soon do we hafta go?" Sam asked.

"It should take your father a couple weeks to close out his business dealings here. We'll put our house on the market right away. Hopefully, it will sell quickly. But if it doesn't, we can stay with Aunt Claudia until it does."

"Good thing it's not right in the middle of the school year," Sam said.

His mother nodded. "In any case, we won't actually leave till you're out of school."

Sam let out a long sigh. "At least there's that, I guess."

For the rest of the evening, the family talked about the great adventure they were about to embark on. In some ways, Sam felt excited about moving to a new place. But he was sad at the same time. *It's gonna be tough leaving all my friends ... the team ... and my school ....* Then he smiled, *wait a minute, I won't miss that place one bit.*

Sam called his friends and asked them to come over.

When they walked through the front door, Tyler said, "Hope you had a nice dinner. We just ate leftovers."

Tony reached over and swatted him on his head. Then he turned to Sam. "What's your big news?"

Sam looked down toward the floor. "I'm afraid you guys aren't gonna like it."

"How come?" Tyler asked.

"We're moving."

Tony grabbed him by the shoulder. "You are not!"

"It's true."

Tyler's voice went into a high-pitched squeak. "But what about our championship team and high school and ..."

"And what about us?" Tony added.

"Hafta leave all that behind. Come on to my room." When they walked in and shut his door, Sam began looking at all his things.

"What are you going to do with this mountain of junk?" Tyler asked.

"Pack it and stack it I guess."

"How 'bout just toss it?" Tyler asked.

Tony walked over and sat on the edge of Sam's bed. "Where you guys moving to?"

"Some place in Louisiana as far as I know."

"What do you think it'll be like to live in a new place?"

"I've been thinking about that. But, I did the same thing when we moved here, and that worked out okay. I like the idea of being near water again too."

"And pirates?" Tony asked.

Sam shook his head. "Don't think so. Those were a long time ago."

"Well, I'd be scared to go."

"So would I," Tyler said.

Sam nodded. "I am too, a little. Except I'll still be with my dad and mom. Nothing bad could happen to me with them around."

"I sure hope not," Tyler said.

That reminded Sam of the scary movie they had watched earlier. And the old haunted house. It sent a shiver straight up his back.

CHAPTER 2

For the next several days, it looked like a tornado had swooped down and only hit the Cooper's house as each family member had to decide what was heading to Louisiana, what was going to friends and neighbors, what would be donated, and what was destined for the dump.

"Why can't I take *all* my stuff?" Sam complained. "I thought we were moving to a great big house."

"We are," his mother told him. "But first, we'll have to put everything in storage."

"It isn't fair, Mom," Sam said.

"A lot of things in life aren't fair."

"Well that's not fair either," he whined.

During the last days of school, Sam did his best to concentrate on the final tests he'd be taking. Thinking about the move made it hard for him to focus. Each time he walked past the trophy case and saw the championship basketball trophy in the center of the case, he stood a little taller. Even though he felt pride in that accomplishment, the thought of leaving Harper's Inlet made him sad. He tried not to show it at school or around home, but he knew people could tell.

Coach Loner met him in the hall. "I heard the news, is it true?"

Sam simply nodded and looked down.

"People are going to miss those three point shots from Sam Cooper, I can tell you that."

Later that day when Sam came home from school, some men from the moving company stopped by to look at all the furniture they would have to move. When they were finished, they gave Sam's mother some papers to fill out and left a stack of flat boxes.

"Sam, I want you to take some of these to your room. Put half of them in our room."

It took several trips, but he lugged all the flat boxes down the hall.

His mother brought a roll of plastic tape and opened the boxes to their full size.

"Start filling your boxes with the things you want to take. Write your name on the outside of each box and what's inside."

"I'll know my stuff," Sam said with a smile.

"Not when all the boxes are closed up and stacked together."

Packing and marking went on for the rest of the afternoon until his father came home from work.

"This place is a disaster," he told them.

Sam's mother smiled back. "That's easy for you to say since you weren't here to help all day."

"I know. Actually, you're both doing a great job."

"I never knew we had so much junk," Sam said. "Every time we move, it's like this."

"Moving is a great way to get rid of stuff."

Almost before Sam could believe it, he took his last test at school, cleaned out his locker, said good by to several of his friends and went home.

That afternoon, his friend, Perry, came over. "I just wanted to thank you again for helping me get back on track at school." He gave Sam a fist bump and said, "And I'll never forget the season we had this year."

Sam shook his head. "Me, neither."

"You're gonna be missed around here. You know that?"

Sam nodded. "I'll miss it, too." He spent the next couple of days going to see many of the people he'd come to know around town in such a short time. He rode his new bike out to the Remmington mansion. As he rolled to a stop, he could hardly believe how great the place looked. He told Mrs. Remmington the news about leaving.

With tears in her eyes, the old woman said, "I'll never forget you, Sam Cooper. Never!"

Sam fought to hold the tears back. "Same here," he said in a trembling voice.

"If it wasn't for you, I don't know where I would be right now."

When Sam left her house, he still felt a lump in his throat. But he knew it wouldn't be any easier when he saw Captain Jack. In fact, he almost hoped the old sea captain would be out on a fishing charter. But as he coasted his bike to a stop at the dock, *My Treasure* was tied up there.

Captain Jack saw him coming and called out, "Ahoy, there!"

Sam took a deep breath and waved. Then he pushed his bike toward the boat. "How's the fishing?" he called out.

"Been great," the captain said. "Come on aboard."

They sat together in the wheelhouse, but Sam couldn't bring himself to look into Captain Jack's eyes.

"I saw your father in town this morning," the captain began.

Sam looked up. "Then you already know?"

Captain Jack nodded. "Can't say I'm too happy to hear it, though."

Sam slowly shook his head. "Can't say I am, either."

"Well, sir, I can tell you one thing."

Sam continued listening.

"You've left your mark on this place. People around Harper's Inlet will be talking about Sam Cooper for years to come."

Sam cleared his throat. "Oh, I'm not so sure about that."

The captain nodded. "You mark my words. And this town is sorry to see you go. I know I sure am. But your new one will be lucky to have you."

Sam stood up, lunged toward the captain and gave him a bear hug. "I'm gonna miss you, Captain Jack."

Now it was the captain's voice that cracked as he held back tears. He nodded. "I know. Now you'd better git."

Tears flowed freely down Sam's cheeks as he rode his bike toward home. Seeing Mrs. Remmington and Captain Jack made the idea of leaving Harper's Inlet even more difficult. Sam kept wondering if there was some way he could stay. But, by now, he'd said his goodbyes to all the important people in his life in Harper's Inlet. He knew it would soon be time to leave, and nothing could stop that now.

The morning came when a gigantic truck rumbled up in front of his house. A smaller van, with more helpers, parked in behind it. Sam's father had finished his business so, for the past few days, the whole family had worked to get things ready. It took several hours for the men to pack everything into their truck.

As the last few boxes were loaded, Sam asked, "Hey, Dad. How do they know if everything'll fit?"

"Some people have so much stuff, it takes two trucks."

"Two trucks? We need *two* trucks?"

"No, we only need the one."

Sam scratched his head. "How will they know where to take all our stuff? I mean, they could just drive off and steal everything."

His father laughed. "We've never had to worry about that before."

Near the end of the day, everything that was supposed to be loaded was on the truck. Sam watched his new bike, given to him by Mrs. Remmington, being wheeled up the ramp. *Wonder if I'll ever see that thing again?*

That night, the family sort of camped out in the den. Each kept a pillow, some blankets, and a suitcase there. They ate supper in front of a small fire in the fireplace. Sam had convinced himself he liked the idea of a new adventure, but as he looked around, he knew he'd miss this house.

"Do we know where we're gonna live, Dad?" he asked.

"Not yet. Mom's sister has some ideas for us. We'll start looking as soon as we get there."

"When *do* we get there?" he asked.

"Since we have to drive the car and the minivan, we plan to break it up into two days."

Tony, Tyler, Perry, and some of the others from Sam's basketball team came over for the last time.

"You weren't here all that long, Cooper," Tony said. "But the place will never be the same without you."

Perry had been holding something behind his back. Finally, he brought a basketball around in front. He held it out to Sam. "Here. This is for you."

"The whole team signed it," Tony said. "Even Coach."

Sam swallowed another lump in his throat. "Man, you guys, thanks."

Then Tyler tugged on his shirt. "Can we talk someplace?"

Sam motioned for him to follow around the side of his house, away from the rest of the guys.

"What'd you want?"

Tyler didn't speak right away. "Well, you know about my mom and dad, right?"

"I know they split up and everything."

Tyler nodded. Then his eyes brightened. "The thing is, I found out they're going to try getting back together again."

Sam tapped him on the shoulder with a fist. "That's great, Tyler. I'm really happy for you."

"I sure wish you didn't hafta go."

Sam nodded. "Yeah, so do I."

By ten o'clock, the Cooper family was on its way. Sam waved to all his friends through the back window as they drove away. The family spent their first night in a motel.

As they drove the next morning, Sam asked, "Dad, our house will be near some water, right?"

"The Mississippi River and not too far from the Gulf of Mexico."

"Gulf of Mexico," Sam said with a sigh. "It goes out to the ocean, doesn't it?"

"Sure does."

Several hours later, the car and minivan drove into a driveway leading to a big brick house with white pillars in the front. Large trees shaded the short lane until it opened into a circle drive.

"Wow! I wish this was *our* house," Sam said.

"It's a nice one, all right."

Before they could get out, a woman hurried onto the porch. She had a wide smile as she shouted, "You made it! How y'all doing?"

Everyone in the family got a hug. Sam tried to hang back so he could miss his, but the woman found him and gave him a great big one anyway.

"This is your Aunt Claudia, my sister. And she's the sweetest girl in Louisiana."

Claudia waved her hand. "Hush, now."

"Where's Ralph?" Sam's father asked.

"He'll be home soon. Come on in."

They walked through the massive house, all the way to a screened porch in the back. When Sam stepped out there, he thought it looked like a whole other house because it was so big. But his eyes quickly found several plates of cookies on the table. His aunt soon came out with a pitcher of sweet tea and glasses.

As he devoured his third cookie, Sam noticed two children standing inside the hallway.

"Scooter … Shelly … y'all come on out here and meet your cousin."

Sam walked toward them. "Hi," he said.

"Hey," Scooter answered.

"Hey, what?"

The boy's face turned red.

"And that's your cousin Shelly."

She smiled back. "Hey."

Sam's father asked, "Are you two enjoying your summer vacation?"

"Yes, sir," Scooter answered, "but it just started.

"Mine too," Sam said.

Sam leaned closer to his mother and whispered into her ear, "They sure talk funny, don't they?"

She didn't answer.

His aunt walked over to Scooter. "After you finish your cookies, why don't you show Sam around the house?"

"Yes, ma'am."

Sam couldn't believe the enormous size of their house. It looked more like a hotel in Harper's Inlet. And he thought it was almost the same size as Mrs. Remmington's mansion. His cousins' bedrooms were bigger than the biggest room in his old house. They each had a high ceiling with a big fan that hung down on a long pole. The windows went nearly from the floor right back to the ceiling. When they walked outside, Scooter showed him where they could play in a grove of pecan trees.

"Is Scooter your real name?" Sam asked.

"No, it's Adam," Shelly giggled.

"Then why do they call you Scooter?"

"My Mom says it's because I didn't learn to walk right away. She told me I kind of scooted across the floor wherever I went."

Sam laughed. "Good thing you didn't sneeze a lot back then."

"Or cough," Shelly added.

"People around here use nicknames a lot," Scooter told him.

"But *Shelly* isn't a nickname, is it?"

"My real name is Michelle."

"Oh."

Scooter looked to Sam. "Maybe we'll have to come up with a new name for you."

Sam wrinkled up his nose. "I hope it's not a dumb one."

"Just don't *do* anything dumb," he told Sam. "Then you'll be safe. Where is your family gonna live down here?" Scooter asked.

"We don't know yet. They hauled all our stuff off in a truck. My dad says they'll keep it someplace till we find a house."

"Well it'll be fun to have you here for a while. There's all kinds of stuff we can do."

"Like what?"

"Do y'all believe in ghosts?"

"I don't know. Never thought about it really," Sam answered.

"Don't you start talking about the old Bourleguard Plantation," Shelly warned.

"Why not? It's a great place to play."

"But Daddy told us to stay away from there."

"He doesn't have to know everything. Besides, people around here say the old house is haunted." He turned to Sam. "I've been just waiting for someone like you to come along so we can find out for ourselves."

Sam gulped as he thought. *Ghosts? A haunted house? Now I'm not so sure I'm gonna like this place after all.*

CHAPTER 3

For the first few days, Sam stayed around the house and did things with his cousins. But since his parents began going out every day to look for a new place to live, it didn't take long for boredom to set in. He and Scooter sat together on the back porch.

"Do you guys ever go down to the Gulf?" Sam asked.

"Sometimes. But you kinda have to go for the whole day. With Daddy working all week, and your parents looking for a new house with Mama, there isn't any time."

"What else is there to do?"

"There's always the haunted mansion."

"But, I thought you weren't supposed to go there."

"Oh, Daddy wouldn't care. It doesn't matter much to him *what* I do."

"How would we get there?"

"Easy. We walk."

"Walk?"

"Sure. It's not that far from here."

"You have a haunted mansion that close to your house?"

Scooter nodded. "But it's been there for like forever. They don't bother us and we don't bother them."

"Who?"

His cousin looked off into the distance. "You know."

That night after supper, Sam and his family took a walk in the trees. They found a place where they could sit and look at the river off in the distance.

"When can we go see some real water?" Sam asked. "I already miss the ocean."

His mother smiled. "One of these days. I promise. But we have to find a home first."

"Any luck yet, Dad?" Sam asked.

"We've seen a few places, but they're all very expensive."

"Too expensive, I'd say," his mother added. Then Sam's mother walked over to look at wild flowers growing nearby.

"Dad."

"Yes."

"Promise you won't laugh if I ask you something?"

"I'll try not to."

"Do you believe in ghosts?"

He gave Sam a strange look, lowered his voice and said, "You mean like the ones that come into your room at night and scare you to death?"

Sam straightened up and stared at his father for a moment. "They do?"

His dad let that idea hang out there for a few seconds before he smiled back. "No, I mean like some people say they do."

Sam relaxed again and breathed a sigh of relief. "I thought you meant something like that could really happen."

"It isn't likely."

"Why not?"

"For one thing, we believe God protects us so there isn't any reason for you to go looking for that kind of trouble."

"What do you mean?"

"I mean, in this world, there is good and there's evil."

Sam nodded. "I know that. We learned about it in Sunday school. But Scooter says there's a haunted house around here someplace."

"Really? I'd like to see one of those."

"You would? Wouldn't you be afraid?"

"Let me tell you something. I'm not sure if ghosts or spirits you can see are real or not. But if you're asking me if they live in a house someplace, I'd say no."

"Why?"

"It's a little complicated, Sam. I believe there are people who have turned their lives over to the dark side in this world. There's no telling *what* those people have seen."

"How do you know there's a dark side?"

"Because the Bible says there is. It tells us we don't have to battle with real people, but we *will* find evil forces that want to get in our way. Especially if we try to help other people."

"That scares me, Dad."

"It's okay to be a little scared. But if you wake up every morning and tell God you need Him to help you in your day … He will."

"I'm trying to do better on that."

"Then, all you have to do is keep trying."

Just then his mother walked over with a handful of wild flowers. "Time to go back," she said.

Later that night, Sam took a little longer than usual to go to sleep. Each time he closed his eyes, all he could see in his mind were pictures of the scariest haunted mansion he could imagine. It had dark windows, broken shutters, peeling paint, and vines that had grown up to cover the door, porch, and tall pillars. He started remembering the sounds of chains from the movie he had watched with Tony and Tyler not long before his family moved to Louisiana. Then he'd blink and see flashing lightning, pounding rain, howling wind, and rumbling thunder.

When he did finally drift off to sleep, the sound and light show started all over again. Only this time, he was sure he heard real thunder. He forced himself to slowly open one eye just in time to see the entire sky light up outside.

"Great," he whispered, "I just get to sleep and here comes a real storm." This one matched some of the powerful thunderstorms he'd seen back in Harper's Inlet. By the time it finished, Sam was exhausted; he slept until the sun came up.

The next morning, Sam and his cousins were once again on their own. Scooter came into where Sam sat on the screen porch in a white wicker chair with large flowery cushions reading a book.

"Your mom make you read like that?"

"No," Sam said without looking up.

"I never read."

Sam turned and looked up at him. "Never?"

Scooter shook his head.

"You should try it sometime."

"I don't think so. You wanna go see the haunted house today?"

"My dad says there's no such thing."

"Is that right?"

Sam nodded.

"Then there's only one way to find out, isn't there?"

Sam closed his book. "You mean ..."

Scooter nodded with a big grin.

"Can your sister go too?"

"Why not? Shelly," Scooter called. A few seconds later, she bounded into the room.

"What'd ya want?"

"Do you wanna go with us to see the old house?" Sam asked.

Scooter rubbed his hands together. "*Haunted* house you mean. If all three of us go together, nothin' can happen."

"You're sure about that?" Sam asked.

"Not a chance."

"Not a chance it will, or not a chance it won't?"

His cousin motioned for them to follow him. The children hurried out the screen door. They walked off through the trees in the direction that Sam and his parents had gone the night before. Then they came out of the trees onto a narrow dirt road.

"Where does this go?" Sam asked.

"You'll see."

"Do any cars drive on this crummy road?" Shelly asked.

"Not many. It's an old back road. We won't stay on it for long."

A few minutes later, they turned and walked off into another field with tall, thick trees.

"What kind of trees are these?" Sam asked.

"It's a pecan grove. This is just one of them on the old plantation."

Sam looked around. "What plantation?"

"Bourleguard."

Sam stopped still. "You mean we're on the place now?"

Scooter smiled at the fear in Sam's voice. "Right now."

"I'm scared," Shelly said.

"Don't worry. It'll be all right," Scooter told her. "We'll go around the front so Sam can see how run down it is."

The children continued through the trees. Broken pecan shells crunched under their feet. Thick brush between the rows made it difficult going at times until they came to a stone fence.

Scooter found a place where they could squeeze through. "It's easier on the other side."

Sam was glad to see there wasn't any heavy brush on that side. Soon they came to a place where the fence turned to the left. The children crept along that part of the rugged rock fence.

"Are you sure there's a house around here?" Sam asked.

"It's there all right," Shelly said. "I've been back here with Scooter a couple times."

Sam looked over toward a second rock fence. "I don't see anything but trees in there."

"A little farther," Scooter said.

There were a few places where other loose rocks had fallen

from the fence over the years. The cousins had to walk around those. While Sam looked down, trying to find the best way to go, his cousin warned, "Sam … look!"

He looked up to see just the roof of a big house hidden back in the trees. "Is that it?" he asked.

His cousin nodded slowly. "This way."

The children inched their way along the final stretch of fence until they came to another dirt road. From there, Sam could see a highway down below. But, when he turned to look the other way, Shelly grabbed his arm and held on tight. "I don't like it here very much," she said.

The cousins stood in front of two towering stone columns on each side of a massive, rusted-iron gate guarding the driveway into the old mansion. Over the top of the gate sat a large, rusted sign that said "Bourleguard." When he stepped a little closer, and pressed his face against the gate, Sam could just make out a huge house with dirty looking pillars along the front. There was a second story with a full porch across the whole floor. Above the porch were more windows indicating the house was three floors in all. Sam noticed the roof had some damage with missing shingles and green moss growing in several places, but the trees blocked most of the house so the children couldn't see everything.

"There's a legend about this place," Scooter said in a hushed voice.

"Legend? What legend?" Sam asked

"He who owns the mansion, owns the treasure."

"You're just makin' that up."

"No, I'm not."

"I've heard that, too," Shelly said.

"What kind of treasure?"

"Pirate treasure." Scooter waved his arms around. "This whole area used to be full of pirates."

"Cut it out," Sam said. "Do you know what this place looks

like to me?"

"No, what?" Scooter asked as he continued looking toward the old mansion.

"It looks just like the house in a spooky movie I was watching with my friends just before we moved."

"What about it?"

"All I can say is if you saw it too, you wouldn't want to take another step closer to that place."

His cousin turned to him and grinned.

Sam held up his hands and shook his head as he tried not to let his voice tremble so Scooter would know how scared he was at that moment. "You don't mean it."

His cousin turned toward the house and nodded as his grin turned to a big smile.

CHAPTER 4

"Let's go in and look around," Scooter suggested.

Shelly stomped her foot. "I'm not going in there."

He turned to Sam. "Maybe we should come back by ourselves."

The children continued peering through the heavy gate. Scooter pushed on it to make it rattle. When he did that, they heard the sounds of barking dogs in the distance.

"Those sound like really big dogs," Sam said.

Shelly began running along the fence. "They're coming to get us," she screamed.

Quickly, the boys hurried off in the same direction. At the corner of the fence, they turned and ran into the trees. After they had run far enough away, Sam stopped and plopped down on a log.

"What are you stopping for?" Shelly asked. "We gotta get outa here."

"I need to rest a minute," Sam said as he struggled for his next breath.

"But the dogs!"

"They don't know where we are. I don't even know where we are."

"I do," Scooter said. "Come on, this way."

When they finally walked back into the yard of his cousins' house, Sam noticed that his parents were back. He ran to look for his father. "Did you find a house yet?"

His father only shook his head.

"People still want too much money," his mother told him. "We're going out again tomorrow."

"But what if you can't find a place, Dad? What then?"

"Then we'll have to change our plans, I guess."

"No bedtime breakfast?"

"Bed *and* breakfast," his mother said.

His father took a deep breath. "We may just have to set our sights a little lower."

Sam studied his father's face. "What does that mean?"

"We've been searching for a place that was nearly ready to go. I think we're going to have to start looking for something that needs a lot of work and where we can do most of it. You know, fix the place up ourselves."

"Like flipping a house?" Sam asked.

"Sort of like that, only we want to live in it too."

"Are there any places around here like that?" Sam asked.

"There've got to be."

That afternoon, the two families decided to drive down and look around New Orleans. The drive took a little over an hour. Sam's uncle had a big van with enough room for all of them. First, they drove out to one of the remaining lighthouses.

"Over the years," his uncle said, "severe storms have devastated many Louisiana lighthouses."

"That one looks like it needs a lot of help," Sam said, after taking a couple of pictures.

"Some preservation work had been started, but after the last couple of storms, most of the money dried up."

"Such a shame," Sam's mother said with a sigh.

Sam kept looking at the lighthouse. "Maybe we should buy

one of those and fix it up for people to stay, like you said."

His mother smiled at him. "Only problem is, who would want to pay money and then have to walk up all those steps to the top just so they could go to bed?"

Next, they drove to the Port of New Orleans.

"Look," Shelly said as she pointed. "I see a cruise ship. You should have your breakfast bed right here."

Sam whistled. "And look at all those other ships."

"Barges too," Scooter added.

"What you're looking at," Uncle Ralph said, "is the world's busiest port complex."

"How do they get all the stuff off those boats and out of here?" Sam asked his uncle.

"The Mississippi River, six railroads, and an Interstate highway."

Sam took a few more pictures of freighters, cruise ships, and barges.

His uncle continued. "Around five thousand ships from nearly sixty countries come here each year. And something like fifty thousand barges travel on the inland waterways."

"How do you know about all that?" Sam asked.

His uncle chuckled. "Because I work down here. We still have some storm damage to the port, but things are getting better."

Sam put his camera away. "What about pirates?"

"What about them?"

"Do you have any?"

"Not anymore, but New Orleans has a rich pirate history."

Sam gulped and then sat quietly.

Later, the families parked in a lot and everyone piled out of the van.

"Where are we going now?" Sam asked.

Aunt Claudia smiled. "Well you can't come to New Orleans and not ride the streetcar."

Again, Uncle Ralph began, "Our streetcars suffered a lot of hurricane damage too. But we can ride them now."

It surprised Sam when he saw the first one. "It looks like the old ones I've seen in books."

"That's what we like about them," his aunt said.

Later, they hopped off and started walking. Uncle Ralph told about how many people say some of the buildings and houses are haunted. Scooter looked over to Sam and just nodded as if to say, *Told ya.*

After dinner, the families walked to a place Uncle Ralph had talked about earlier. They came to a stop when he pointed and said, "This … is Pirate Alley."

Sam gulped but couldn't say anything. He thought he'd left stories about pirates and treasure behind him when they'd crossed the Florida state line.

His uncle continued as they stepped into the alley, "Some people claim that this was a meeting place for pirates. But there's a church on one side and a dungeon on the other."

"A real dungeon?" Sam asked.

His uncle nodded. "I doubt many pirates would have spent much time between a dungeon and a church."

"Yeah," Scooter said. "That'd be dumb."

Uncle Ralph pointed and said, "One of the ghost stories comes from this place."

"Ohhh," Shelly said. "Tell it, please, Daddy."

"They say that Reginald Hicks and Marie Angel Beauchamp wanted to get married, but their families wouldn't approve. The only person they could find to perform the ceremony was a minister who, unfortunately, was in jail."

The children moved in a little closer.

"Well, he went ahead and married them anyway. Mr. Hicks had been raised by pirates."

Sam shuddered. "Real pirates?"

His uncle nodded. "That's what the story says. Anyway, they

were married, but had to keep the marriage a secret from Marie's people. No one knows what happened to him for sure, but some say he died in the Battle of New Orleans."

"Then what happened?" Sam asked.

"They say he may have left with the pirate Jean Lafitte."

"I've read about him in school," Sam said.

"And you'll hear about him all over Louisiana. The thing is, people say Hicks still comes back to the alley. In the early morning, on the right day, at the right time, you'll hear laughter from a wedding, the sound of bells, and a chilly breeze blows right through you."

Just then a gust of wind swept down the alley. Shelly screamed, but no other sounds were heard.

Sam decided, even though he was a little afraid, he was going to like his new home a lot … except for all this talk about ghosts, strange sounds, and haunted houses. Up until now, he only heard about stories like that around Halloween. He turned and looked at his father, who simply shrugged his shoulders. As they left the alley, Sam made sure to look inside every building and window he could, just to be sure.

By the time they returned to his cousins' house, it was late and the families went straight to bed. Again, Sam didn't go to sleep right away. He wondered why everyone around this place was so interested in ghosts. But deep down, he really didn't want to know too much more.

When he finally did fall asleep, he was restless. He kept having wild dreams that included the movie he and his friends watched on the day he found out about moving. Suddenly, his mind transported him inside the old plantation house his cousin had shown him. He saw thick cobwebs hanging everywhere. A musty smell filled the place and several of the wooden stairs leading to the second floor were broken, rotted, or missing. Cold damp air made him shiver. The dream caused him to roll around in his bed for most of the night.

When morning came, he was relieved. After breakfast, his parents were off again with Aunt Claudia to look at more houses. When they left, Scooter asked, "Wanna go back to the old plantation today?"

"I don't know. I didn't sleep too well last night. And what about Shelly?"

"That's okay. She went to a friend's house to play girl stuff all day. We'll be on our own for a change."

Sam didn't really want to go back to the old place, but he didn't want to seem like a chicken either. "I guess it'll be okay."

The boys slipped out the back door and headed the same way they'd gone before. The farther they walked, and the closer they came to that frightening mansion, the more afraid Sam felt. But he didn't let his cousin know about that, or the weird feeling he had in his stomach.

Soon they stood at the old, rusted gates just like before. A thick blanket of clouds covered the sky this morning, making the mansion look even more frightening.

"This place is spookified," Sam whispered.

"What are you whispering for?"

Sam let a nervous laugh slip out. "Yeah. Funny, isn't it?"

"Let's go closer."

"You crazy? What about the dogs we heard?"

Scooter cupped a hand behind his ear. "Do you hear them now?"

"No."

"Well, then?"

Sam took a deep breath. He was just about to follow his cousin when he saw something and pointed. "What's that?" he whispered.

"There you go whispering again."

Sam kept pointing toward a rusted object on the ground, covered by a clump of Spanish moss. His cousin reached down, brushed the moss away and turned a sign over. "It says 'No

Trespassing'."

"That means we aren't supposed to go in there," Sam said.

"How could it?" Scooter held the sign up. "If they wanted people to stay out, this sign would still be up on a post or something. If it's in the dirt, that must mean they don't care anymore."

Sam shook his head. "I don't know."

His cousin tossed the sign into nearby bushes like a helicopter. "It doesn't matter what you do, but I'm going in." He squeezed between the two big gates then turned back to Sam. "Well?"

Just after his cousin pushed through, Sam heard the sound of big dogs barking again in the distance.

"I've heard those lots of times," Scooter said, "but never seen any dogs around here."

Sam put his lips together and forced out a heavy breath. His heart pounded a little harder and deep inside, he didn't feel good about what he was about to do. Still, he pushed through too and joined his cousin inside the gates. "What now?"

"We go closer, take a look around and get back out of here."

The old mansion looked even worse the closer they went. Sam could see shutters barely hanging on their rusty hinges. Large sections of the house didn't have any paint on them and the columns were cracked and crumbling. Several windows were broken or missing. He looked up to see those missing shingles on the roof when something terrible happened.

High up in one of the windows on the third floor, he was sure he saw the face of a man dressed in a black robe. A hood covered his head, but there was no mistake, Sam saw his chalky, white face. For a moment, Sam froze and couldn't move. He wanted to say something to his cousin, but he was unable to force the slightest sound to come out. With a trembling hand, he reached out to tap his cousin on the shoulder.

When he did that, Scooter jumped right off the ground. "What did you do *that* for?"

"I ... I ... I."

His cousin glared back at him. "You ... you ... you what?"

"I ... I saw something."

"What?"

"I'm not sure, but I think I saw a man's face up in that window."

"Which one?"

Sam pointed to the cracked window in the center of the third floor where he was sure he had seen someone. Just then a curtain moved, but there was no face.

"Probably the wind," his cousin said.

"What I saw was *no* curtain."

"Oh, I'm so sure."

No sooner had Scooter said that than they began hearing the sound of chains being pulled across a hard wood floor someplace high up in that old house.

"Let's get outa here!" Scooter yelled. By the time he said "here," he was already running at full speed toward the gates. Then Sam heard the dogs once more, only they didn't seem to come any closer as he ran to catch up with his cousin.

The boys skidded to a stop, squeezed through the main gates and dashed to some nearby bushes. They dove underneath them, then turned around to see what might happen next. But nothing did.

"What was that legend again?" Sam asked, gasping for breath.

"He who owns the mansion, owns the treasure."

"Wonder what that means?"

"Yeah. Wonder?"

CHAPTER 5

The boys ran all the way back home without taking a break or resting for even a second. When they opened the door to the porch, Scooter reached out and grabbed Sam by the arm.

Sam pulled away. "What'd you do that for?"

"I wanna show you something. Come on to my room."

Sam followed him. Once inside, his cousin shut the door. "What is it?" Sam asked.

Scooter shook his head. "If I show you, you have to promise not to tell anyone else … not even your parents."

"That depends on what it is. I mean, if you're doing anything bad or it could get me in trouble."

His cousin shook his head again. "No, it's nothing like that. I just mean we have to keep it a secret." He stared right into Sam's eyes. "Promise?"

Sam thought about it for a moment, then nodded. "Promise."

We gotta spit shake," Scooter said."

Sam cocked his head to one side. "What's that?"

His cousin spit into his own hand and looked to Sam. "Now you do it too."

Sam wasn't sure exactly what was going on, but he raised his hand and spit. Then his cousin put his hand out and said,

"Shake." Their hands slapped together and then slipped apart again. Sam wiped his hand on his pants and Scooter did the same.

"Now what?" Sam asked.

"There are a lot of strange stories around where we live. They talk about ghosts, pirates, treasure, and all kinds of spooky stuff."

"And you believe them?"

Scooter walked over and sat on the edge of his bed. "I think some are true, and I don't know about the rest. All I know is I found something that could be worth a lot of money."

"Is this another one of your wild ghost stories?"

Scooter shook his head and looked toward a bookcase in his room. "Something much better than that."

"Well, what is it?"

"You promised, right?"

Sam nodded.

"And we spit shaked, didn't we?"

Sam nodded again.

"Okay, then." His cousin stood up and walked over to his bookcase. He pulled a stepstool from the corner, placed it in the middle of the case and stepped up. Then he raised his arms as high as he could, reached in and pulled out an old book. Sam noticed other books that looked just as old. Scooter brought the book down and took it to a desk under his window. In the bright light, it was clear this book was older than any Sam had ever seen before. It had yellowed pages with worn corners and the leather cover looked dull and cracked.

"Where did you get that?"

"My mom loves garage and yard sales. She's all the time bringing home junk, and it drives my dad nuts. So, one day she brought home these old books in a box she bought for ten bucks." He pointed to where the other books sat on the high shelf. "She thought they'd look great in my room, so she gave them to me."

Sam looked at the book on the desk. "What'd you do, look

this one up on the Internet and find out it's worth a million dollars or something?"

Scooter shook his head. "Even better."

Sam's eyes widened and his eyebrows went up. "Better than a million dollars? This I gotta see."

"It's not about the book," Scooter said. "It's what I found inside."

"Money?" Sam asked.

"No."

"Some old stocks and bonds?"

Scooter shook his head.

"I give up. What is it?"

His cousin opened the heavy leather cover. Inside, the pages looked as if they might crumble if Scooter wasn't careful. He slowly turned the pages until he came to the middle of the book.

There, Sam saw a wrinkled, brown paper folded in two. "Is that it?"

In a hushed voice, his cousin answered, "Uh-huh."

"What *is* that?"

Scooter sat down and carefully took the paper out, set the book to one side, opened the folded paper and spread it out on the desk. "I'm pretty sure it's a treasure map."

"Oh, come on!" Sam said in disgust. "I got spit all over my hand for that?"

His cousin looked up at him.

"I'm sure there are thousands of those all over Louisiana, and they're all fakes."

"What makes you say that?"

"Because, people used to make up treasure maps and sell them to other people who didn't know any better. There never was any treasure except for the money they made selling the maps."

Scooter held up his map. "But this one is really old. It has to be real."

Sam shook his head. "All that proves is it's *real* old."

Scooter placed the map back on his desk. "Look closer." He pointed to some of the lines drawn on the map. "Right here looks like where the river turns, see?"

"That could be any river anywhere."

"Then what about this?" His cousin put his finger on something that looked a lot like the mansion they had explored earlier. "I think this is the same place we were exploring."

Sam leaned down and looked closer. Then he shook his head. "It still doesn't prove there's any treasure."

"My mom said the people she bought the books from have lived here all their lives. They got the books from their relatives and the books go back a long, long time."

"But if it's a real map," Sam began, "then how come no one else has ever searched for it. And if they did, who says they didn't already find it and spend all the money?"

Scooter let out a long, deep breath. His shoulders sank. "I never thought about that. But then, why would anyone hide a map in a book for all these years? It doesn't make any sense."

Sam shook his head. "All the talk around this place about ghosts, pirates, treasure … it's enough to make people crazy."

Scooter held up the map again. "Well, don't you think it's at least worth looking around the mansion again?" He pointed to the spot on the map showing a mansion with several odd marks dotted around it. "What if there really is treasure buried on the old Bourleguard place?"

CHAPTER 6

After dinner that night, Sam's father had gone out to check a couple things on the engine of their minivan.

Sam walked out to find him. "What's wrong with it?" he asked.

"Nothing, really. I just haven't had a chance to look at the fluid levels on our cars since the trip up here."

"Can I help?"

"Sure. Hold this light for me, will you?"

Sam took the flashlight and aimed it where his father pointed. "You know a lot about cars, don't you, Dad?"

He laughed. "Just enough to be dangerous. For the big things I need a *real* mechanic. Hand me the funnel over there. And that extra rag, too."

Sam found them, then aimed his light again. "And you know about lots of other stuff, too."

"To a guy your age, I probably seem like the smartest man in the world." He chuckled. "But that'll change when you get a little bit older."

"Well, the other day we were talking about ghosts and stuff."

"I told you to be careful with those things, remember?"

Sam nodded. "I know. And it isn't like I'm going out of my

way to look or anything."

"What's the problem?"

Sam thought for a moment, then cleared his throat. "Suppose a guy thought he saw something, only he wasn't sure?"

"What was it he thought he saw?"

"Maybe a …"

"Ghost?"

Now Sam felt a little more nervous than before. He accidentally shined the light into his father's face.

"Hey! That's too bright."

"Sorry." Sam tilted the flashlight down again.

"Where did he think he saw this … ghost?"

"In a haunted house."

His father stopped what he was doing, wiped his hands on a rag and looked up. "I know they told us on the tour that some of those places were haunted, but that isn't real."

"What about the ghosts?"

"Well, *I've* never seen one. I do believe there are angels."

"You do?"

His father nodded. "But how many angels have *you* seen?"

Sam smiled. "None."

"Even so, I believe they're real."

"Then what about all the witches and stuff we see on TV or in books?"

"All part of how crafty the devil is. He gets to run a lot of things here on Earth, but he isn't more powerful than God. You have to keep that in your mind and not worry. It's the people who go looking for trouble who find it."

"But that ghost I thought I saw?"

His father straightened up. "You saw?"

"Forget I said that."

"You can tell this *guy*, maybe it was something else and his mind played a trick on him."

"Some trick," Sam said with a nervous laugh.

"Let's finish this up before it gets totally dark, and I start pouring oil all over my feet."

On the way back to the house, Sam asked, "Are we going to find a church around here?"

"It's the next thing we plan to do as soon as we know where our new house is."

"How come Scooter's family doesn't go to church?"

"That's something we hope to change."

"Well, he believes ghosts are real."

"I'm not surprised."

"How come?"

"Let's just say he doesn't know as much about the things you learn about in church."

They began walking toward the house again. "Why not?"

"It isn't that important to a lot of people."

"I'm sure glad it is to us."

His father put his hand on Sam's shoulder. "So am I."

When they returned to the house, the rest of the family sat out on the porch. Another big pitcher of sweet tea sat in the middle of a table. Next to that was a bowl of ice cubes and next to those, Sam saw two more glasses. He and his father each took one, clinked ice into their glasses and poured cool tea into two tall tumblers. Sam quickly took a big gulp.

"It's a hot one tonight," Uncle Ralph said.

"Sure is," Sam's father answered.

"Y'all going out again tomorrow to look for a place?" Scooter asked.

"Got to."

"Have you narrowed it down any?"

"A little."

"Hey, Mama," Scooter said. "Can me and Sam sleep out here on the porch tonight with the fans on us?"

Sam turned to his cousin, but he didn't like the odd look he saw on Scooter's face.

"I don't see why not," she said.

After they'd had peaches and ice cream, the parents went inside to get ready for bed. Shelly went on to her room. Sam and his cousin pulled cushions off the wicker furniture and made beds on the floor. But Sam still had an uneasy feeling.

Scooter's mother brought out sheets and pillows. "Remember to brush your teeth before bed," she told them.

"Yes, ma'am," Scooter said.

When the boys came back out on the porch, it surprised Sam to see Scooter climb into bed. He settled into his too.

"You gonna leave that light on all night?" Scooter asked.

Sam turned and looked at a lamp in the corner. It was still on. "Oh, I thought …"

"Last one to bed turns out the lights."

Sam crawled back out and switched off the lamp hanging by a chain from the high porch ceiling. As he returned to his bed again, he felt the breeze from two big ceiling fans over his head.

"I like the way you have fans in every room here. Back home, we just had an air conditioner."

"We have one too, but Daddy only uses it on the really hot days."

"And this isn't one of them?"

"Oh, it gets a lot hotter than this."

"It does?"

"Uh-huh." After being quiet for a little while, Scooter asked, "So what'd you think of my old house?"

"Creepy."

"I know. That's what I love about it."

"You do?"

"I can't get enough of that scary stuff."

"I can."

"You just don't know what you're missing."

"And I don't want to know."

His cousin switched on a table lamp next to his bed. "Tell me about the face you thought you saw over there."

"I'd rather not think about it."

"Come on, tell me."

"It was a man's face. He wore a black robe with a hood. I saw him up on the third floor … in one of those little windows."

"Cool."

"It isn't cool. My dad says things like that are bad for you."

"You mean real live ghosts?"

"They aren't real."

"Oh, no? So how do you explain the one *you* saw?"

Sam shook his head. "I can't."

"Then I have an idea."

"I'm afraid to ask."

"If you're so sure they aren't real, why don't you prove it to me?"

"How?"

"I say we both go over there and find out."

"You mean now?"

Scooter nodded and smiled. "Right now."

"But …"

"But nothin'. If they aren't real, then you got nothin' to worry about."

"And if they are real?"

His cousin growled and rubbed his hands together. "Yeah."

CHAPTER 7

The boys slipped out the back door and into the darkness. Sam didn't like it much, but he also didn't want anyone to think he was still a baby. And what if he could prove that ghosts weren't real? Wouldn't that be a good reason for Scooter to start going to church with him? That thought helped him make excuses for thinking what they were doing was all right.

Yeah, I guess that's a good reason to be doing this.

Like two tomcats hunting in the night, the boys slinked off through the trees. Sam hadn't expected how easily he could see where they were going because of the full moon. But the farther they walked away from the safety of Scooter's house, the closer they came to danger, Sam felt.

About halfway there, something fluttered into a tree just above Sam's head.

"What was that?" he whispered.

"Probably just a dumb bird or a bat."

Then something else darted between his legs.

"That was no bird," he complained.

"Stop worrying. It's only a swamp rabbit. See." He pointed to a set of tall ears on a mound nearby.

"We really shouldn't be doing this."

Scooter just ignored Sam and kept walking. Twice, they tripped on brush and fell. In the distance, Sam heard the mournful sound of a boat's horn out on the river. It gave him a chill.

The boys continued walking until they came to the stone fence. They had to feel their way along until Scooter located the break.

"Here it is."

They each slipped through. Again, it was easier to walk on that side of the fence, especially in the dark. At the corner, they rounded the fence and crept toward the gates.

"You ever been here at night before?" Sam whispered.

Sounding brave and confident, his cousin said, "Sure, lots of times."

"Ever seen anything strange … at night?"

"Saw it and *heard* it."

Sam stopped. "Heard what?"

"All kinds of moaning, some crying, and the chains. I really don't like the chains."

That made Sam shiver. He quickly rubbed both arms to make the goose bumps go back down. "Those chains are the worst. Where do you think the noises come from?"

"Ghosts, what else?"

Sam reached out and grabbed the sleeve on Scooter's shirt. "I think we should go back."

"Look, in all the times I've come over here, sometimes by myself, sometimes with other guys, nothin's ever gotten me. Now come on."

They walked a few more steps when Sam asked, "You said you've heard and *seen* things. What kind of things have you seen?"

"Lights and stuff mostly. You'll see."

Way too soon for Sam's liking, they'd found the entrance. As the boys stood outside the heavy gates, the place looked scarier at night than in the daytime. It was even worse that any movie Sam could think of. All it needed now was some kind of spooky music to set the right mood. Sam decided it should be a giant pipe organ and that's the kind of music he heard in his head. It went perfectly with the full moon that sat just above the chimney on the right side. As Sam looked up at it, something dark fluttered right across the center of the bright moon.

"Did you see that?" he whispered.

"See what?"

"Something just flew across the moon."

"Probably another bird … or a bat like I said."

Sam shuddered again. His cousin squeezed through the gates but Sam stood on the outside. "What about the dogs?"

"That's the strangest thing. I almost always hear them, but I told you, I've never seen one. Besides, dogs can't climb trees, and we can if we have to."

Don't let this be the night we have to. Then, he slipped through the gate and joined his cousin on the dangerous side. They edged their way along a row of trees, making sure to stay off the dirt driveway.

As they moved closer to the old mansion, Sam stopped, grabbed Scooter by the arm and pointed to an upstairs window. "What's that?" he barely whispered.

The boys watched as a lamp moved from the center window on the third floor, disappeared, and passed across the next one. Then it went out.

"It's like I told you, sometimes I've seen lights in there."

Sam gulped. "It almost looked like the light went right through solid walls from one room to the next."

They only took a few more steps when suddenly, Sam heard barking from the most ferocious dogs he had ever heard. It sounded like the roaring beasts might be about to charge right toward them. Quickly, the boys jumped up into the nearest tree. Once they'd climbed high enough so no dog could possibly reach them, they each sat on a branch. But no dogs ever came near them.

"I don't get it," Sam said. "I thought dogs could smell a guy no matter what, even in the dark. I've seen it in movies where a guy's trying to break out of prison or something. A guard lets the dog smell a shirt that belongs to the escaped prisoner, and the chase is on. It doesn't matter if the guy runs fast, climbs a hill or even a tree like us up here, the dogs still catch him. Unless he runs through a creek or something."

"See, that's like I told you. You hear dogs but never see them. They must be tied up or in cages, and all they do is warn whoever's inside."

Sam and Scooter climbed up a few more branches. From high up in the tree, they had a clearer view of the house. They couldn't have been more than twenty yards from the front of the old place. Just then, another light appeared on the second floor. From there, it seemed to float down all the way to the main entrance of the house. Sam wished he'd stayed back in his safe bed on the porch. He grabbed onto a branch and held on so hard, his hands began hurting. But if he thought he'd been scared up to this point, it was nothing compared to what happened next.

As he watched in terror, the light drifted right up to the inside of the double front doors. They heard a loud click. Then one of the doors slowly began to open. The old, rusty hinges made a screeching sound that split the night air. As the door opened wider, the eerie light came clear out onto the front porch. Then it stopped.

Sam looked closer as three dark figures stood there. Suddenly, another light came on up in one of the third floor windows.

Both boys heard an evil laugh. Then that light went out. While Sam and Scooter had been watching up there, the three dark figures *on* the porch had come *off* the porch. Sam could hardly breathe as they now walked straight toward the tree where the boys crouched on branches. Sam began shaking so hard, he was sure the leaves would start rustling and give away their hiding place.

"I think I'm gonna be sick," Sam whispered.

"I'm about to wet my pants," Scooter said.

"Watch it!" Sam said. "You're right above my head."

The dark figures seemed to almost float across the ground until they stood directly below the boys' tree. They moaned, then swayed back and forth. Next, they walked in a circle around the base of the tree several times. The dark figure holding the lamp continued raising it into the air, then lowering it back down.

Suddenly, they stopped walking.

This time, when the light came up, Sam saw the face of the man holding it—the same face he'd seen in the window. Terror gripped Sam's chest. He couldn't blink, swallow, or breathe. Just when he thought he might faint and fall right out of the tree, the dark figures laughed together. Then, they seemed to float back toward the house just as they had come out. And as they moved, the dogs began barking again.

Sam couldn't remember the last time he'd taken a full breath. He breathed in deeply, then slowly let it out. "That … is … the … *scariest* thing I have *ever* seen," he whispered.

"Me too," his cousin barely squeaked.

"I thought you saw stuff like that all the time over here."

"Never this close up."

"Let's climb down and get outta here before they come back."

The boys scurried to the bottom branch, then dropped to the ground. As soon as they moved, the dogs began barking again.

"Come on!" Sam yelled as he sprinted toward the gates and safety. His cousin ran right behind him. Once on the other side, the boys hurried to the nearby bushes again, dove behind them and hid.

Sam gasped for breath and shook so hard, he could barely speak. "Wh … what do you think that was all about in there?"

"I told you, the place is haunted. Has been as long as I've lived here. Everybody knows it. And most people stay away."

"Most *smart* people you mean." He continued to gulp for air.

Sam and Scooter watched as strange lights continued moving inside the house, but the dogs soon quit barking. After they were sure it was safe, the boys crept out from the bushes and started toward Scooter's house. On the way, Sam imagined he saw creatures and shadows behind every tree, just waiting to jump out and pounce on him. Suddenly, he walked into something that completely covered his face.

"What is *that*?" he squealed.

Scooter took out a small flashlight and shined it into his cousin's face. "You just walked into a clump of Spanish moss and some spider webs."

"Man, I was sure one of those ghosts had me." Sam quickly brushed the moss off his face and shirt.

The boys didn't talk anymore until they were safely in bed back on the porch.

After several silent scary minutes, Sam asked, "How many times have you been over there at night?"

Scooter didn't answer right away. Then he cleared his throat, waited a few more seconds and said, "This was my first time."

"Liar!"

"No, honest."

"I mean you lied when you said you went over there all the time."

"It's true … just not at night."

"Why not?"

"Because my sister's too scared, and I never had anyone else brave enough to go with me before." His voice began to trail off. "I've only heard the stories."

"You *were* scared!"

"Weren't you?"

"I sure was," Sam said. "But, I thought you'd seen the lights before."

"I've only been around when older kids talked about them.

It's a big thing around here for guys to show how brave they are. I'm not sure how many of them who say they've done it really have." He was quiet for about another minute. "We should go back."

"Now?"

"No, not now. In the daytime, again. I'd feel safer then."

"Are you nuts?"

"We can take Shelly with us."

"Now I *know* you're crazy."

"There's something about that place," Scooter said.

After a nervous laugh, Sam said, "No kidding."

"I mean it. We need to go back for a closer look."

That thought gave Sam a sick feeling in his stomach. "I don't care if I never see that old broken-down mansion again as long as I live.

CHAPTER 8

The next morning, Sam heard strange noises inside Scooter's house. He slowly pushed the door open. What a relief when he walked into the kitchen where his father asked, "You and want to go with us today?"

"Where?"

"To look at a couple houses, have lunch, things like that."

"Sure."

After breakfast, they piled into the minivan and drove off. It was the first time the family had been able to spend time together since they arrived.

Sam's mother turned around and said, "After lunch we're going on a tour."

Sam smiled back.

Before the family could have lunch, they needed to look at a few houses that might make a good bed and breakfast. Each place had three stories.

Just like the haunted mansion, Sam thought.

Two of the houses were completely white with black shutters on all the windows. The properties displayed beautiful gardens, swimming pools, rocking chairs on the porches, and large shade trees. The family didn't go inside any of the houses. Sam's parents told him they had already done that with a real estate saleswoman.

"We wanted you to help us pick one out after you saw the trees and yards," his mother told him. That was just before they came to the most beautiful place Sam had ever seen. Up until then, he thought most of the houses looked pretty much the same. Those were mostly white, with black roofs and brick walkways. Sam looked out the window as they passed a house big enough to be a hotel.

"What about that one?" he asked.

His father threw back his head and laughed. "That's the most expensive house we've seen yet."

"At least, it shows you have good taste," his mother added.

"But, it's the nicest house I've ever seen." Sam's eyes drifted across a front yard that looked more like a well-kept golf course. This house had tall white pillars like many of the others, and it also had three stories. But there was one big difference. The house was made completely out of brick.

"It reminds me of the three little pigs," he said.

"Huh?" his father asked.

"All the other houses we saw are made out of stuff that might fall apart. But I don't think you could ever blow that big brick house down. Why can't we buy that one, Mom?"

She smiled. "We can't seem to afford that one or any of the others you've seen today either."

"What are we gonna do, Dad?" Sam asked.

"Have to change our plans a bit I guess."

"What's that mean?"

"It means we keep looking until we find something that doesn't cost quite so much. Now, who's ready for lunch?"

Right away, Sam said, "I am."

They drove down toward the port. Their van came to a stop in front of a seafood restaurant. The family walked inside and, for the next hour, they enjoyed an all-you-can-eat fisherman's buffet. Sam put mostly shrimp on his plate.

Back at the table, his father asked, "Did I ever tell you the joke about another all-you-can-eat restaurant?"

Sam shook his head. "No, but I'm sure you're about to."

He smiled. "Seems there was this salesman who had been on the road all day. He hadn't made too many sales and he was running a little short of cash."

"What did he do?" Sam asked.

"He only expected to get a bowl of soup and a crust of bread when he noticed a sign that said, 'Roast Beef Dinner, all-you-can-eat for five dollars.' Well, this was perfect, the man thought. He screeched his car to a stop and hurried in. 'I'll have the all-you-can-eat dinner,' he told his waitress. Soon, she came back holding a small plate with an even smaller scrap of meat and a pitiful pile of mashed potatoes with only a tiny drip of gravy on top. 'What do you call this?' he asked. 'I thought the sign said I could have all I could eat for five bucks.' His waitress looked down at his plate and said, 'You're right. And that's all you can eat in *here* for five dollars.'"

"He should sue them for false advertising," Sam said.

After dinner, the family decided to walk for a little while. Sam's mother told him, "We thought you would enjoy another guided tour."

"What kind of tour?"

"Just a walking around more of the historic buildings."

"That sounds kinda boring."

"We're trying to learn as much as we can about the area," his father told him.

"Do we hafta?"

"You might like it."

"I doubt it."

Soon after the tour began, Sam heard something that changed his mind right away.

"It wasn't long ago," the guide told them, "that a group of

treasure hunters found another cannon that may have been from a pirate ship."

"Did she just say pirate?" Sam asked in a whisper. His father only nodded.

"Was Lafitte a real pirate?" someone asked.

"Oh, yes. Very real. And there were many more in this area. Divers have also found gold dust, broken bottles, and a few plates out in the Gulf."

"Do they think there's treasure, too?" another asked.

"Well they aren't diving out there for the fun of it," she said with a smile. That made everyone laugh.

"A lot of treasure?" Sam asked.

"It's possible. Many pirates used to sail these waters. Legend has it that treasure is still buried up and down the coast, just waiting to be found. Some of it is even rumored to be hidden farther inland."

Sam didn't need to hear another word. Even though the tour continued, all he could think about was treasure, Scooter's map, and the mansion.

That is, until this guide also said, "Pirate Alley is well known for its pirates, haunted buildings, and ghost stories."

Sam stopped walking. He remembered the story his uncle had told.

The guide began. "We had an old lighthouse out on one of the islands. Legend has it that the keeper and his young daughter moved into the family quarters. That lighthouse was built because violent storms blew in, often without warning. The lighthouse helped ships and boats get back into port safely. Well, one day it was time for the keeper and his daughter to come into port for supplies. They were always careful to travel only in daylight and when the weather was calm. They set out on that morning in their small rowboat. After a beautiful day in town, the keeper and his daughter headed back to the lighthouse in their little boat, loaded down with supplies."

"What happened?" a girl's quivering voice asked.

"A strong wind blew up, and dark clouds quickly formed."

"Did they turn around and go back to town?"

"No. They hurried toward the lighthouse. It was the keeper's job to make sure the light was burning to warn ships of danger. But the waves grew larger as the wind howled. Then suddenly, waves came over the side, the boat filled with water and sank. The keeper strapped his daughter on his back and began to swim. He must have passed out because he couldn't remember making it to the shore of his island. But when he awoke, he was cold. Yet, he felt his daughter still strapped to his back. Only she felt even colder."

"Oh, no," a small voice said. And that gave Sam a chill.

"His beautiful little girl had drowned. Even today, sailors tell of a pretty little blonde girl who appears on their decks, almost always when the weather is still. She points toward land and begs them, 'Go back!' This always happens just before a terrible storm. And as the legend goes, any sailor who ignores her warning and goes out into the ocean is sure to die there."

Several people in the group whispered to one another about what they had just heard.

"Do you have any more ghost stories like that?" Sam asked.

"Plenty of them," she said. "A young woman planned to marry a sailor. The only problem was, her father forbade them to see each other. Bu,t the woman and the sailor continued to meet in secret. Then suddenly, he stopped coming to see her. The woman's heart was broken. Still, each night she put a light in the window so he could find her house when he returned from the sea. But he never did. Many years later, neighbors found her, an old woman by that time, dead in the upstairs of her big house. People around here said she died of a broken heart."

"Then what happened?" a woman asked.

"The house has had lots of owners since then. Some said a ghost lives in the attic of that old house."

Sam heard gasps from several of the people gathered around their guide.

"Strange noises, like chains dragging, have often been heard along with an eerie light shining from the attic. It was as if the ghost of this woman was still trying to signal to the sailor she loved."

Scooter and I saw lights in the attic of the old mansion. I wonder?

The final stop on the tour took them to Jean Lafitte's Blacksmith Shop. "It was built before 1772," the guide told them. "People say that the ghost of Lafitte is often sighted inside. Some have claimed that they saw the pirate sitting in the dark."

"Really?" Sam asked as his body shuddered.

"When they look again, he's gone. Others tell of red eyes glowing from the fireplace." The group moved to another corner of the building, and the guide continued. "Fishermen have reported seeing a ghostly fleet of ships in the Gulf while others claim they've seen a pale man, dressed in black, standing on the back of their boat. Many legends insist that Lafitte's gold has lots of hiding places, depending on who's telling the tale. They say he has his gold hidden all over south Louisiana, that his pirate ghosts guard it, and many believe Lafitte is coming back for it some day."

Sam could hardly blink as he wondered about everything he and Scooter had heard and seen.

CHAPTER 9

When they returned to his cousins' house, Sam went looking for Scooter.

"You aren't going to believe what I heard today."

"I might."

"No, you won't."

Scooter grinned. "What was it? That ghosts live all over and lots of places around here are haunted?"

"How did you know that was it?"

"I live here, remember?"

"But people talk about ghosts like they're your next-door neighbor."

"They are."

"Are not."

"You got any better explanations?"

"My dad says it's because people want it to be real."

"I want them to be real."

Sam just looked at him. He'd never heard anyone say something like that before. He sort of thought everyone grew up in a family like his, even though he knew that wasn't true. "Doesn't it bother you?"

"Doesn't what bother me?"

"You know."

"Hey, if it makes you happy to believe in God, then you just go right ahead and believe it. I like to think there are all kinds of more important things to think about."

"Well, I know one thing. Ghosts aren't real. They can't be."

"Oh, yeah? Then why don't you try and prove it?"

"Prove it? How?"

"By coming back to the haunted mansion with me. I'll show you who's right and who's wrong."

"But I don't ever want to go *near* the place again."

"You still scared?"

Sam nodded.

"Then the best thing to do is go back, and I'll prove I'm right or you can prove I'm not."

Sam's body stiffened. "But we're not going after dark. That is the creepiest place I've ever seen."

"We should get Shelly to go with us again."

"She won't want to," Sam said, "I can tell you that right now."

"I'll ask her."

"I'm telling you she won't go."

"But if she says yes? I mean, you don't want a girl to go, and you're too scared."

"Oh, all right. I'll go then."

Later that night, Sam's sleep was interrupted by one bad dream after another. First, he dreamt about that old woman who died in her house. Then, his mind switched to the little girl in the water. After that, he had a terrible dream about the haunted mansion. In it, he saw himself being pulled into the attic. When he woke up from that dream, his whole body shook with fear and his sheets were all tangled. *I really don't want to go back to that awful place.*

Just as he almost fell asleep again, he heard a strong wind begin blowing. It seemed to come out of nowhere. He rushed to the window to see small branches falling from the trees along with streaks of lightening in the distance. That made him think about the little girl in the bay, and he shuddered once more.

It took a long time, but he finally went back to sleep. The next morning, all four parents planned to look at houses again. The cousins told them they'd be okay, and they wanted to stay around the house.

After their parents left, Sam and Scooter hurried to find Shelly who was playing on the porch.

"You wanna go back to that stupid old mansion again today?" Sam asked.

"Sure," Shelly said right away.

Sam turned to Scooter. "Did you already talk to her?"

"About what?"

"Never mind. Let's get going."

Scooter and Shelly scampered off the porch toward the old house, but Sam was in no hurry to get there. They had to keep waiting for him to catch up. Finally, all three cousins stood at the front gates. While the others pushed through, Sam waited outside.

"You comin' or not?" Scooter asked.

"I really don't like this place."

"What's not to like?"

"Have you told Shelly yet?"

"Told me what?"

"Well, me and Scooter came over here late the other night ... by ourselves."

"You *did*? In the dark?"

Sam nodded. "We heard the dogs like the ones barking now. And we saw some other stuff."

"Like what?"

"I'd rather not say, except we had to climb into a tree to hide."

"Hide from what?" Shelly asked.

"There were these three creepy guys," Scooter told her. "They came out of the house in black robes with hoods over their heads."

Her mouth dropped open for a moment. "What did they do?"

"They glided right over to the tree where we were and started floating around it in a circle."

"I'm gettin' out of here," Shelly said and started toward the gate.

"You can't go," her brother told her. "We have to stay together. Besides, it's daylight now. That happened in the dark."

"Yeah, and now we want to find out who or what that was," Sam added.

"As long as you big strong boys are here," Shelly said, "I guess it'll be okay."

Strong boys ... ha ... if she only knew.

The children used the line of bushes along the lane leading up to the house as a hiding place until they came to the front yard. Sam looked up into the third-floor window once more ... and there it was. "Look!" he cried. But when the others looked up there, the face was gone.

"Look at what?" Shelly asked.

Why is it I'm the one who doesn't believe in ghosts, but I'm the only one who can see them?

The children crept onto the porch and slipped up to the front door. Scooter put his hand on it. The door clicked and began opening all by itself. Sam took a half step back. The door creaked like something deep in a damp dark dungeon.

"We've come this far," Scooter whispered.

As they slipped inside, the children heard chains dragging across the floor right above their heads.

"There they go again," Sam said.

"Could we get out of this place?" Shelly cried.

"Just stay close to us," Sam said. At that moment, he was sure he'd felt a pair of eyes looking at him from a large, dark painting of a man just above the fireplace. But when he glanced back, they looked like painted eyes again. In silence, the children began walking up the stairs to the second floor.

A thick layer of dust covered the steps and woodwork. Sam noticed large footprints in the dust on the stairs. He pointed to them. "Look," he whispered. "No kids made those."

A loud thump sounded from the third floor. When they came to the top of the first stairs and turned to go down the hall, Sam walked into a mass of spider webs. "Get 'em off me! I hate those things."

His cousin helped him clear the webs from his face and neck. Then, the boys picked up a couple of broken sticks from the floor and used them to clear a path through the rest of the webs. Soon, they came to a large window looking out over the back yard.

"Look down there," Sam said. The children peered out through dirty windowpanes to see hundreds of small holes that had been dug in the ground. "Must be a thousand gophers in that yard."

"Not gophers," Scooter said.

"What then?"

"Remember the legend?"

"What legend?" Shelly asked.

"It says, he who owns the mansion, owns the treasure."

"Treasure? I remember that," Shelly said.

That's when a low, scary sounding voice thundered, "Get … out … of … my … house!"

"Don't ask me twice," Sam yelled as he dropped his stick and bolted toward a back stairway. But before he started down, Sam saw something. The others quickly followed until they all stood in the kitchen. The cousins turned to go back toward the front when they heard loud thumping out there.

"Not that way," Scooter said. "Follow me."

They raced out the back door, sprinted across the yard and through another break in the stone fence. The children ran until they were at a safe distance again.

"That is the weirdest place in the whole world," Shelly said as she tried to catch her breath.

"It's haunted, that's why," Scooter added.

Sam folded his arms defiantly. "It's not haunted. And I can prove it."

CHAPTER 10

"What's this big proof you got?" Scooter scoffed.

"Just before we ran down the stairs, I saw somebody."

"You mean you saw a ghost?"

Sam shook his head. "I saw a *real* man."

"How do you know that?"

"Because I saw him standing in the shadows of the hallway. And we both saw those big footprints on the stairs, too, remember?"

"Sure, I saw them. So what?"

"I think there are real people in there trying to scare everybody away."

"Why would anyone want to do that?"

"You said it yourself, 'He who owns the mansion, owns the treasure.'"

Scooter scratched the side of his head. "I don't get it."

"We're going back there."

"Now?"

"No, later. Tonight, after it gets dark."

"And what if the place *is* haunted?"

"It's not. You'll see."

"I *hope* you're right."

"Can you get a cell phone?"

Scooter nodded. "I already got one."

The boys arranged to sleep on the back porch again. Not even Scooter's sister knew what they were planning. At around midnight, Sam and Scooter slipped out the back door, making sure to close it without making a sound. Scooter brought along his small flashlight. But the moon again provided most of the light they needed to find their way through the pecan trees.

When they came to the place with a break in the fence, Sam said, "Not that way."

"Why not?"

He motioned for his cousin to follow. "I'll show you."

As quiet as swamp rabbits, the two dark shadows made their way toward the back of the property. As they came near, Sam's heart began beating harder. *I sure hope I'm right*, he thought. When they stepped into the clearing of the back yard, he whispered, "Notice anything different?"

"Yeah. We aren't at the front gate."

"Not that. Something else, listen."

His cousin thought for a moment. Then he shook his head.

"Hear any dogs barking?"

Scooter smiled slightly. "Hey, you're right. How come?"

"I'm not sure, but I have an idea." He crept over to a trash pile and picked up two metal garbage can lids. Next, he found a couple of big sticks and handed a stick and a lid to his cousin. "Right now, no one knows we're here."

"How can you tell that?"

"Come on, you'll see." They crouched down and moved closer toward the back door, making sure they couldn't be seen. Like before, the door wasn't locked. The boys eased through, crouched down and walked like a couple of mice to the back stairs. They climbed to the second floor, then crept to the staircase leading up to the third floor.

That's when Scooter reached out and grabbed Sam's sleeve and stopped him.

Sam shuddered all over. "I *wish* you wouldn't do things like that," he whispered.

Scooter pointed up toward the darkness. "But ... you aren't planning to go up there?"

"I sure am. And when we get there, I'll give you a signal. When I do, you start pounding on your trash can lid as hard as you can with that stick."

Scooter looked down at what he held in his hands. "What good will that do?"

"You just watch and see."

Sam turned and put his foot on the first step. The old wood squeaked as soon as he put any weight on it. He stopped, turned to his cousin and put a finger to his lips, "Shhh."

Scooter shook his head and whispered back, "You're the one making all the noise, not me."

Each step in this final staircase made some sort of sound as the cousins climbed higher. They finally made it to the landing at the top of the third floor. Just ahead of them stood a heavy, wooden door. Sam chose his next steps carefully as he eased himself up to the door, put his ear to it and listened. "Just what I thought," he whispered. He dropped to his knees and peered into a large keyhole under the doorknob.

Scooter leaned down and asked, "See anything?"

Keeping his eye to the keyhole, Sam nodded. Then he stood up, stepped back a few steps, looked to his cousin and yelled, "Now!"

The boys started beating on the metal lids as hard and as fast as they could. It sounded like the drummers leading a marching band across a football field. Then, Sam began making ghost sounds. And Scooter did that too. If they'd stopped to think about what they were doing and listened to themselves there in the dark, it probably would have scared them to death right where they stood. But what they heard next almost made them stop banging on the lids and start laughing. That's because of the terrified screams from what sounded like at least four people on the other side of the door. Next, they heard two of them crash into each other and fall to the floor.

"I'm gettin' out of here," a man hollered. "This place really *is* haunted!" Then, the boys heard the men stumblin', tumblin', and rumblin' down the back stairway in the dark.

Sam raised his clenched fist in the air. "I think I just bowled a strike."

"Spare me," Scooter laughed.

Sam reached out for the doorknob, grabbed and then slowly turned it. The latch clicked, the hinges screeched and then the door swung open. Sam had seen a little of the room through the keyhole, but what the boys saw next even Sam hadn't expected. It looked like they were standing in the control room of a television station. Sam had visited one of those on a field trip before his family moved to Louisiana.

Video monitors lined the wall, and they were still turned on. Sam noticed four beds along another wall. Their covers were strewn all over the floor. He looked a little closer, laughed and pointed. "Looks like they forgot their shoes."

"That's gotta hurt," his cousin said.

"They left a lot of papers and other stuff too. Better take your phone and call nine-one-one."

"What for?"

"The police. There isn't supposed to be anyone living in the place. I think they'd like to know about this."

Scooter dialed the number and handed the phone to Sam. He heard, "Nine-one-one, what's your emergency?"

In a nervous voice, Sam answered, "Me and my cousin are in an old, abandoned mansion. It has a no trespassing sign and everything. There are big trees all over, it has a stone fence and iron gates."

"I know where that is. It's the old Bourleguard place. But if it says no trespassing, why are you in there?"

"We came to investigate."

"Investigate what?"

"To see if it really was haunted."

"And what is your emergency?"

"Well, these guys are living in it ... on the third floor. They've got all kinds of video equipment up here and a control room. There must be cameras all over the place."

"Now, son, it's against the law to make a prank call to nine-one-one."

"It's not a prank. They really were here."

"I'll send some officers out there right away. But you keep talking to me and stay where you are."

Then Sam realized what he had just done. He knew he and Scooter were in big trouble now. He turned off the phone, spun around toward his cousin and said, "We better run ... now!"

The boys hurried downstairs, around to the back way and out into the night. As they ran, they heard sirens in the distance from several approaching police cars. Now Sam wished he hadn't called them, but it was too late for that. Sam and Scooter raced all the way home as fast as they could, sneaked up on the porch and crawled into their beds. It took a long time until they stopped breathing like race horses from their long run and their big scare.

"What do you think's gonna happen?" Scooter asked.

"Well, the cops were right behind us. I think they'll find all that stuff on the third floor and take it out."

"Then what?"

"Then that should be the end of it. We'll be heroes ... only we won't ever be able to tell anybody about it."

"Why not?"

"Because the police told us to stay there, but we didn't, and because we weren't supposed to be in there in the first place."

"We could really be in trouble, couldn't we?"

"I don't want to think about that right now," Sam whispered in the dark.

Just then, the boys heard a phone ring inside the house. *Who calls in the middle of the night?* About a minute after they heard that sound, it looked like every light in the house came on. Then all four parents rushed out onto the porch.

"Would you boys like to tell us what you've been up to?" Uncle Ralph asked.

"Nothin', Daddy. Honest. We've been sleeping out here the whole time until you came out and woke us up right now." He stretched, yawned and rubbed his eyes; pretending to still be almost asleep.

"Whole time? What do you mean, whole time?"

"I mean ..."

"Sam?" his father asked.

Sam looked down and didn't answer right away. Then he said, "We weren't sleeping. We just got back."

Scooter glared at him. "We did not!"

"Back from where?"

Shelly stumbled out onto the porch. "What's going on?" she asked as she rubbed her eyes.

But before anyone could answer that question, the doorbell rang. As the families moved cautiously toward the front door with the boys trying to hide behind their parents, Sam saw flashing lights coming from the driveway.

CHAPTER II

When Uncle Ralph turned the lock and opened the door, there stood two of the biggest police officers Sam had ever seen. Shelly quickly hid behind her mother and held onto her arm, tight.

"Is this the Welty residence?" one of the men asked.

"Yes, officer, it is. What seems to be the trouble?"

The other police officer looked beyond the parents to the boys. "Oh, I think someone here can tell us the answer to that question."

In a squeaky voice, Scooter asked, "How did you guys find us anyway?"

Sam turned to his father. "We snuck out tonight."

"Where?"

"We went over to that haun … that abandoned house."

"What house?" his mother asked.

"It isn't far from here. Scooter showed us."

"Us?" she asked.

"All three of us kids went over there."

"When?"

"A couple times."

"You took a girl with you to an empty old house?" his father demanded.

Sam simply nodded.

"So why are the police here?" Uncle Ralph asked.

Sam turned to his cousin. "You wanna tell 'em?"

Scooter cleared his throat. "It has these signs around the fence that say 'no trespassing.' We didn't think they meant anything because the stone fence was broken down and you can squeeze right through the gates."

"Those signs are there for a reason, son," one of the policemen said. "Old houses like that can be dangerous places."

"Tellin' me," Sam sighed.

"But I still don't get how you guys found us," Scooter said.

"One of you boys made a phone call, right? To nine-one-one?"

Both boys nodded.

"And when you did that, the number registered in our call center. All we had to do was look it up, get the name of the owner and here we are." He smiled down at them.

"Whose phone did you have?" Uncle Ralph asked.

"Mama's. My battery died."

"Adam! You took your mother's cell phone without permission?"

Scooter nodded again.

"We can talk about that later."

Scooter just stood there and kept quiet.

Then the other officer asked, "What can you tell us about the four men we caught running down the road?"

"You got 'em?" Scooter asked as he smacked a fist into his hand.

"We sure did. And you know what was the oddest thing?"

"What?" Sam asked.

"Not one of them was wearing any shoes. They almost begged us to put them in the squad cars."

"Why?" Shelly asked.

"Because their feet were so cut up and bloody from running

across broken pecan shells. I don't think they could have made it much farther."

Then the second officer laughed. "They kept telling us the place where they'd been hiding was haunted or something."

"That was us," Sam told them. "Did anyone go upstairs into the third floor?"

The officer shook his head.

"Well, we need to take you up there tomorrow. You won't believe it."

They agreed to meet out at the old place around three the next afternoon. Then the police left. The parents talked with the boys for the next half hour. Then everyone went back to bed. But neither Sam nor his cousin could go to sleep right away.

"We must have busted up something important," Scooter said.

"I'm not sure *what* it was. But at least we know those goons won't be coming back to scare the wits out of us ever again."

"I still say the place is haunted."

Sam sighed. "You're impossible ... you know that?"

The next morning while the families were still eating breakfast, the phone rang. Uncle Ralph answered it. "It's for you," he told Sam's father.

He went to the phone. "Hello. Yes, we can be ready by ten. Sure. Okay. We'll see you there. Thank you. Goodbye." Then he hung up.

"Who was that?" Sam's mother asked.

"The real estate office. She got the key we wanted. We can meet her at the office, pick up the key and have a look on our own."

"A look at what?" Sam asked.

His mother began, We looked at pictures of a house yesterday. We knew we couldn't get through the gate without a key so, we only saw it online. There were some big trees hiding it in the pictures, but the agent says it's just the perfect place for us, and in our price range."

"It's going to need some work," his father added. "And we expect you to help us get it in shape for our first guests."

"This is *very* exciting," Shelly squealed. Sam rushed to his room to get dressed. A few minutes later, he raced down and the family drove off. First, they stopped at the real estate office. Sam's father hurried back out with a ring of keys in his hand.

"Doesn't anyone have to go with us?" Sam wondered.

"No," his mother told him. "They told us no one is living there right now."

After they had driven a little longer, Sam's father pulled the car over to the side of the road and stopped. "Since this is such a big surprise, we want to put a blindfold over your eyes until we get there."

After Sam had his on, he joked, "You'd better hope the police don't see me like this. They'll think I got kidnapped or something."

"Remember, you and Scooter have a date with the law later today."

Sam's shoulders drooped. "Don't remind me."

The car started out again and drove on a smooth road for a few more miles. Then, Sam felt the tires drop off onto a rough road. The trip became bumpier after that. Finally, they came to a stop.

Sam reached to open his door. "Can I take it off now?"

"Not yet."

His parents each took an arm and led him from the car. Sam heard his father open a lock and a chain fell to the ground. Next, he heard a sound like a large metal door opening. Then, they walked for what seemed like a long time. In the distance, dogs barked. Sam tripped a couple times and almost fell once. Finally, they came to a stop.

"My, my," his mother said. "This place looks worse up close."

"Can I see it now, Mom ... *please?*" Sam begged.

Slowly, his father removed the blindfold. But when Sam looked out, he couldn't believe his eyes. He stood in stunned silence for the first few seconds. "Not *this* place," he sighed.

"What do you mean, *this* place?" his mother asked.

Sam began to sputter. "It's ... I mean ... um ... it ... it's ..."

"What are you trying to say?" his father asked.

"I'm trying to say that this is the haunted house me and Scooter have been talking about."

His mother turned to him. "You mean *this* is where you were last night?"

Sam nodded.

Then, his parents burst out laughing. "It better *not* be haunted," his father said with a gulp. "This is going to be our new home."

"You're kidding," Sam said. "Have you guys been inside?"

"No. That's why we had to get the gate key."

Sam let out a deep breath. "I have, and you don't need any more keys. It's a big mess in there."

Sam's mother looked back at the mansion. "I don't understand."

"Dad," Sam barely managed to say. "Wait till you see what's on the third floor."

He led the way as they stepped through the front doorway and began looking around. A thick layer of dust still covered everything. Dark red curtains hung in the living room. A few pieces of old furniture remained scattered in the house, but most of the rooms were empty. Sam looked at the old painting above the fireplace. Now it just had two holes where the eyes should be.

From a second-floor window, he showed his parents all the digging in the back yard.

"Where did those holes come from?" his mother asked.

"Looks like a big piece of Swiss cheese," Sam joked.

"Scooter and I haven't been here long enough to dig *that* many holes."

"Then who?" his father asked.

"Has anybody told you about the legend?" Sam asked.

His parents looked at each other, shook their heads and turned back to Sam.

"Scooter told me there's a legend about this place."

"What does it say?"

"He who owns the mansion, owns the treasure."

"That probably just means that if you own a big place like this, that's treasure enough," his mother told him.

"I don't think so. Because those guys who were in here were trying to keep other people away."

"But why?"

"You heard the guide who told us all those stories about ghosts and pirates. Maybe there's buried treasure … right on this place somewhere."

His mother smiled and put a hand on his head. "You have such an imagination."

"*Imagination*? Follow me to the third floor. I didn't imagine what's up there."

CHAPTER 12

Sam led his parents up the narrow stairway to the door where he and his cousin had pounded on the trashcan lids. Those were still on the floor where the boys had dropped them in the dark. When he pushed the door open, his father walked in and let out a long, loud whistle. "What is all this?"

"It's the control room those guys were using."

"But, why?" his mother asked.

"I told you. They were trying to keep everyone off this place. And I think they're the ones who dug up the back yard."

His father took a card out of his shirt pocket and then dialed a number on his cell phone.

"Officer Daniels, please." He waited for a moment. "Yes, sir. I wonder if you and some of your men could come out to the old house a little earlier?

"Why? Because we're here now and there's something we need to show you.

"Good. We'll see you in about an hour." Then he ended the call.

Sam had been looking at the monitors when he spotted something on the control panel. He picked up several pictures. "Will you look at that," he said.

"Look at what?" his father asked.

"These pictures. I'm even in some of them."

"What pictures?" his mother asked.

Sam gave her a stack. Then he asked, "Can I run over and get Scooter? He's gonna want to see these."

His father looked up. "Okay, but make sure you're here when the police come."

"I will," he called back over his shoulder as he hit the stairs. He ran all the way to his cousins' house. When he reached there, he found Scooter washing one of the cars.

"You hafta come with me back to the mansion?"

His cousin took a soapy sponge and started scrubbing a front fender. "Can't," he grunted. "Gotta wash the cars."

Sam reached out, grabbed the sponge and dropped it back into a bucket. "You can do that later."

"No, I can't. It's part of my punishment, thanks to your stupid idea of calling the cops."

"But you have to come. My dad asked for you, and the police are coming over right now. They want to talk to both of us. Tell your Mom and hurry." Then Sam spun around and hurried back toward the mansion.

Right after he stumbled inside, all out of breath, his cousin charged in the back door of the old house right behind him.

"What's the big hurry?" Scooter asked.

"Wait till you see what I found."

They rushed up the stairs without stopping all the way to the third floor. When they burst into the control room, Sam's parents stood there, still going through the pictures.

Sam grabbed another stack off the control console and handed them to his cousin.

"Hey," Scooter said, "There's pictures of us in here."

"I know. Now do you still believe in ghosts?"

Scooter didn't answer. "Here's one of us at the gate. And look, here's a couple of night-vision ones of us climbing that tree."

Sam slowly nodded as he looked at the pictures. "I wondered how those guys knew to walk right up to the tree where we were hiding and go around it like that. They even kept pictures of it."

Sam looked up. "What's that?"

Scooter's eyes got bigger. "I hear those dogs barking,"

Both boys searched the monitors. One of them showed a picture of two police cars coming through the gates.

"Oh, that's it," Sam said. "I wondered how they did it."

"Did what?" Scooter asked as stared at the video monitor.

"Knew whenever we were coming up to the house, except for the last time when we went in the back way."

"How'd they know?"

"Just watch. As soon as those cars come up to the house, I'll bet the dogs stop barking."

They waited until the cars came to a stop. That's when the barking stopped, too. As the officers stepped out, a different dog started barking.

"Motion sensors," Sam said.

"You think so?" his father asked.

"I'm sure of it." He hurried down to show the police how to get to the third floor. One of them brought a video camera to record everything. While they were still working, the family went downstairs to look at the rest of the house.

"Are you really thinking about buying this place?" Sam asked.

"We'd still have to borrow some of the money," his father said, "but it just might work."

"Work? It's gonna be a *lot* of work," Sam groaned. "Just cleaning up all the dust and fixing broken steps will take days."

His mother smiled. "It kinda reminds me of the Remmington place back at Harper's Inlet. Seems to me you fixed that old house up like new again. Wasn't it as bad as this one?"

"Yeah," Sam said, "but don't forget, we had all that donated material and an army of people helping us."

Just then, a scraggly little black dog peeked around one side of the doorway. Sam saw him first. "A *dog*! Can we keep him?"

"He must belong to someone," his mother said.

"But he doesn't have a collar or anything, and look how skinny he is. Shouldn't we feed him or something?"

"If he decides to hang around after we move in, he can stay," Sam's father told him.

"I always wanted a dog," Sam said. "We just never stayed in one place long enough to keep one." Sam knelt to the floor and held his hand out. The dog looked at him for a few moments, then slowly moved through the door toward Sam, keeping his head down. When he got a little closer, his tail began wagging. Sam started scratching the dog's ears. "I'll bring food over for him … every day."

After a while, the police packed up to leave. "We have all the evidence we need for now. As far as we're concerned, if the equipment up there isn't stolen, you can keep it, Mr. Cooper."

Sam's father nodded. "Make a great security system for our bed and breakfast."

"Is that what you plan to do with the old place?"

"Yes, sir."

"It'd be nice to see the old mansion all fixed up again."

Another officer turned back from the front door. "Well, just make sure you get all the proper permits from the county. This place has been neglected for a long, long time."

"We will."

Scooter had to get back home to finish washing the cars, but Sam and his family continued looking around the house. Sam even found a secret place behind the fireplace, where he could look out through those eye holes from the back of that old painting.

Later, he said, "Dad, it has so many rooms. I wonder who used to live here?"

"We can check the county records to find out some of the history. I think our guests would like to know some of that too."

"The family was probably here from before the Civil War," his mother added.

As they walked into the kitchen, she took a deep breath. "This room needs the most work."

"This and the bathrooms," Sam's father said.

"Do you think there ever were any ghosts here, Dad?"

"We've talked about that already. I don't believe they exist. You've even seen for yourself how real people tried to make others believe there were ghosts here."

Sam continued listening.

"Do you think those men would have spent one night in this place if there were any *real* ghosts?"

"I never thought about that. And they sure took off when we made all that noise."

Just then, a terrible scream came from the second floor followed by the slamming of a door. Sam looked around and couldn't see anyone else anywhere.

"Who's there?" he called out, but no one answered. The rest of the family ran upstairs and began looking in the rooms. Finally, Sam found his cousin Shelly in one of the large bedrooms. "I didn't know you came over, too," Sam said.

She put a hand to her mouth and giggled. "I'm sorry. I followed Scooter but he didn't know it either. I was up here looking around this room. Then, when I turned around, I saw this little girl staring at me."

Sam's stomach tightened.

"Where? What little girl?" Sam's father asked.

Shelly pointed to the closet door. "In there." She opened the door and showed them a tall mirror leaning up against the wall inside. Then, she giggled again as she pointed at her own reflection. "There she is." The rest of the family laughed along with her.

But soon, it was time to leave. Sam put the little black dog outside. Then he hurried around to make sure all the doors were closed. As they walked toward the gate, he heard the sound of dogs barking again. *Some dogs.*

Sam's parents drove back to the real estate office the next day to sign papers for the old mansion. For the next several days, Sam and his parents worked together to begin cleaning up the old place. Most of the things in the house had to be thrown out. They kept some of the old curtains and furniture. But no one could sleep there yet.

"Where we gonna get stuff to fill up all these rooms, Dad?" Sam asked.

"We've come up with a plan at the bank. Because we expect to have paying guests once the house is back in shape, we can borrow money to buy beds, fix things, and get it ready."

The little dog continued to come back to the house every day. And each day, Sam brought him something to eat.

"I thought up a name for him," he told his mother.

"What is it?"

"I'm calling him Spooky."

"That's a funny name."

"Hey, Dad, what do you think about naming this dog Spooky?"

"If he reminds you that there aren't any ghosts, it's fine with me."

"Then Spooky it is," he said with a smile.

Spooky barked twice, wagged his little tail, and whined.

CHAPTER 13

With all the talk about ghosts, pirates, and treasure, Sam wanted to do a little Internet research. He took a break from working on the mansion and went back to his cousins' house where Scooter let him use a computer. There, he searched for information about the most famous pirate Louisiana had ever known. Sam knew his name was Jean Lafitte.

"What can you tell me about Lafitte?" Sam asked Scooter.

His cousin stretched out across the end of his bed. "Well, I know there's a town named after the guy not far from here."

Sam turned around, "There is?"

"Yeah, you can look it up."

Sam entered the information, clicked on a link, leaned forward and began reading, "Not long after the founding of New Orleans in 1718, the French explored the area and established Barataria Bay as a harbor for large ships. Barataria started showing up on maps in 1729. By the 1730s, early colonists settled in the area. Barataria means dishonesty at sea." He turned around to his cousin. "This doesn't say anything about the town."

"Just keep reading."

Sam returned to the computer screen, scrolled down and began reading again. "In 1808, brothers Jean and Pierre Lafitte organized a group of smugglers and privateers, and set up their headquarters on a barrier island." Without turning back, he asked, "What's a privateer?"

"I don't know. Look it up," Scooter grunted as he rolled over on his stomach.

Sam searched and read out loud, "A privateer is an armed ship that is privately owned and manned, commissioned by a government to fight or harass enemy ships." He turned around to his cousin again. "Was he a pirate or something else?"

Scooter shrugged. "That's what I've always heard."

"I wanna know more about the guy."

Scooter slid off the bed. "Fine, but I just got out of school and I'm not looking to take history again in summer school now." He left the room and shut the door.

Sam continued his search. He found the pirate was born in 1780 and died in 1823. He and his brother smuggled and pirated goods in their new port at Barataria Bay until the American navy invaded the area and captured all of Lafitte's ships. In exchange for a pardon, Lafitte and his men helped General Andrew Jackson defend New Orleans against the British. Lafitte and his men were praised by the Americans for their skills which were greater than those of the British. Then Lafitte and all his men were granted a full pardon for their service. Later he moved to Galveston, Texas, where he and his men took several Spanish ships in the Gulf of Mexico. He was believed to have died in a battle with a heavily armed Spanish ship and was buried at sea.

After about an hour, Sam leaned back in his chair, rubbed his eyes, stretched and took a deep breath. "But what about his buried treasure?" he said.

Just then Scooter came back into his room. "Can we go out and do something?" he begged.

Sam shook his head, leaned forward and clicked on another link. "Not yet, I'm just coming to the good part. This guy says there are rumors about buried treasure all along the coast of

Louisiana. And some other guy got sent to prison for taking money from people and telling them he knew where the Lafitte treasure was buried. Did you know about that?"

"Why do you think I showed you my map?"

Sam shook his head. "And that's just it. That guy was a fake, and so is your map probably."

"But my map's so old. It has to be real."

Sam looked back at the screen. "Just because it's old doesn't mean anything. This guy went to jail way back in 1909. What if he made your map?" He found that a private search for Lafitte's treasure took place in the 1920s where water was drained, and a search was made.

Scooter let out a deep breath of disgust.

"Listen to this," Sam said. "There are so many legends about buried gold in Louisiana, all a person needs to do is pick up a shovel and start digging." He spun around to his cousin. "Hey, do you think that's what's those guys were doing at the mansion?"

Scooter shrugged like before.

Sam read again. "There are at least thirty tales of buried treasure. The problem is which of the thirty are worth exploring?" Then Sam's eyes fixed on the next line. For several seconds, he couldn't blink and he didn't take a breath. His voice cracked with excitement when he read out loud, "Who can say for sure that Jean Lafitte, pirate king of kings, who set up his headquarters just off the Gulf Coast, didn't leave his loot there or someplace along the Mississippi bluffs near Baton Rouge—perhaps as much as eleven million dollars in gold?"

When he heard those words, Scooter lunged toward Sam and the computer, nearly knocking him out of his chair. "Let … me … *see* … that!" Scooter read the same line to himself.

Then Sam took over reading again. "Even if it's possible that most of Lafitte's loot has been discovered, many other finds have been made in Louisiana."

"They could be talking about my map, there," Scooter said, pointing at the screen.

Sam read on, "One report says a man and his son found over two hundred thousand dollars worth of old coins, jewelry, and silverware in Louisiana. They used a metal detector. A farmer plowed up an iron pot filled with a thousand gold coins."

Scooter stood and read over Sam shoulder.

"And listen to this," Sam said. "In 1929, twenty-one Spanish doubloons were found in a load of gravel at the Louisiana and Arkansas Railroad tracks in ... get this ... Baton *Rouge!*"

Scooter tapped a finger on the screen. "Look at all the other places where people have found treasure around here and all around New Orleans."

Sam glanced at the time. "Whoa, I gotta get home."

"Hey," Scooter said, "I was hoping we could find something to do, but you wasted all that time on my computer."

Sam smiled as he stood up. "Maybe it wasn't wasted."

Chapter 14

When Sam noticed how Spooky brought up a newspaper every morning, he thought he'd found himself a pretty smart dog. The next time he saw his father, Sam asked, "When did we start getting a paper?"

"What are you talking about?"

"The paper. Spooky brings it up to the house every day."

"He *does*? But ... we don't take a paper."

"We don't?"

"We're going to have to find out where that little pirate is stealing them from and make him stop it."

The next morning, Sam's parents needed to meet a man at the bank to sign some more papers. They decided to take Sam along. He sat out in the waiting room, but he could still hear what was going on in the office.

"Well, Mr. and Mrs. Cooper, it looks like everything is in order."

"Our loan was approved?"

"Yes, sir. You can get the repairs done to the roof and purchase some of the furnishing and appliances on your list."

"That's wonderful," Sam's mother said. "But, we need so much money to fix everything."

The banker laughed. "Maybe you'll be lucky and find the treasure."

"You know that's only a story," Sam's father answered.

"All I know is people have been digging around out there ever since I first came to town. And that was over thirty-five years ago."

"But, it's just a legend," Sam's mother said.

"You mean, 'he who owns the mansion owns the treasure?'"

Sam's heart jumped. He couldn't believe his ears. This wasn't his cousin talking. It was no guide. This man worked in a bank with a big office and everything. *Maybe it is true.*

—⟋⟍—

That night, he talked with Scooter. "I'm telling ya, the guy at the bank said the same thing you did about the treasure."

"Well, I told you I didn't make it up. I've heard that my whole life."

"Yeah, but you heard about ghosts your whole life too and look how that turned out."

"They could be real. I'm still scared of 'em."

Sam thought for a moment. "You know, we found a church we've started going to. You should come with me sometime. I've got a really nice teacher for my Sunday school class."

"Class? The farther I can stay away from school for the summer, the better I like it."

"If you came with me, maybe you wouldn't be so afraid of ghosts anymore."

"I'll think about it."

Several times, Sam's aunt and uncle came over to paint and hang wallpaper. Aunt Claudia helped Sam's mother pick out the colors, material for curtains, and all the rugs.

"Your mom really knows what she's doing, doesn't she?" Sam said.

Scooter shrugged his shoulders. "She used to charge people because she was a pro at it. But she doesn't do that much anymore."

A large stove had been delivered and was now hooked up in the kitchen. The families often used it to make pizzas while they were working. Then, they'd sit around and talk as they ate.

"This place is really coming along," Uncle Ralph said. "How long before you'll be welcoming your first guests?"

Sam's father swallowed. "We have to finish it first. Then we can take a bunch of pictures and start advertising on the Internet, and even with mailings, I think it might still be a while."

"Are you planning to tell haunted-house stories like some of the other bed and breakfasts?"

He shook his head. "Probably not."

"Draws quite a crowd of loyal guests. Some places even have haunted weekends with all kinds of scary events, especially around Halloween"

"I don't think so. But thanks for the ideas."

"Well, why not?"

"We want to give people a place where they don't have to think about those kinds of things. If they have questions, we'll be happy to tell them more."

"Sometimes we have questions," Aunt Claudia said.

"You can ask us anytime."

"Maybe we'll do that," she said with a smile.

"Anyway," Sam's father continued, "we were sort of thinking about having your family as our first guests."

"How nice," Aunt Claudia said.

Then, everyone went back to work on the house. By now, the entire downstairs level had been redecorated. All the furniture was in, and Sam thought it looked good enough to be a movie set. He knew that next week, the movers would bring their own furniture out of storage and set up the part of the house where his family would live.

One of the guest rooms looked like a giant dollhouse. The wallpaper had bright pink and green stripes. Puffy, white curtains decorated the windows. The hardwood floors sparkled and the furniture had been painted in yellow, pink, green, and white.

Shelly flopped in the middle of the four-poster bed. "I feel just like a big doll," she said.

Sam's new room had been newly decorated to look like an old ship with a big captain's wheel at one end. When he looked out his window, while standing behind that wheel, he imagined himself as the fiercest pirate, with the fastest ship, who ever threatened the Gulf of Mexico.

I wonder what it was like for people to sail out there with old wooden ships. Now, he wished he'd grown up in Louisiana like his cousins.

His father helped him start a garden in the back yard. They bought a used garden tractor with a small plow on the back. Sam's father taught him how to use it, and Sam started getting the dirt ready for planting. After he completed that job, his father told him, "Why don't you take the tractor and start filling in all these holes in the back yard. The grass should start growing back, and we'll have a beautiful yard for our guests."

That job took Sam most of the week. *What if I dug up the treasure with my tractor? If there is any treasure. Wouldn't that be something!*

But, he could see why people would want to stay there after they finished all the work. His father hired professional painters to paint the big pillars out front and the rest of the outside of the house. They also used their equipment to paint all the shutters black. Now, the house looked like many of the others Sam had seen in the area. The long driveway set their house apart. Coming through those beautiful trees, guests would feel like they'd entered an enchanted world. Sam sure did.

It wasn't long before some of the plants in the garden began popping their heads out of the ground. Sam had only played around with seeds in science class before. This time, he was growing real food and herbs.

One day, while he worked in a back room, he heard his parents talking.

"We'd better get this place together as soon as we can," his mother said to Sam's father.

"I know. It feels like the money wants to run out before our paying guests ever start coming."

"How much longer do you think it'll take?"

"About five weeks."

"Five weeks?" she asked. "Are you sure?"

"I think so. We can start working on some of the promotions and take a few pictures though. It's looking like we'll be ready by fall."

His mother sighed. "I sure hope so."

"Me too."

Their voices sounded more worried than before. That made Sam worry a little, but he didn't tell anyone how he felt. He just started working even harder and faster to help get things ready in time.

A few evenings after his work was done for the day, he'd go up to the third floor and play with some of the video equipment. Spooky followed him wherever he went. Sam's father had asked him to make a list of what was in the room, how many cameras were in the system, where the sensors and speakers were located and to make sure everything worked. If he found any broken equipment, he was supposed to put that on the repair list.

One afternoon while he was up there alone with Spooky, he heard the barking dogs sound from outside. He checked the gate monitor and noticed a car driving up the lane. He pushed the toggle switch on the remote control to that camera and followed the car all the way to the circle drive. Two men stepped out and walked toward the front door. Sam switched to that camera next. He saw his father come and let them in. He decided to hurry downstairs and see what was happening.

"We're the county building inspectors," one of them said.

Sam's father nodded. "Yes. We've been expecting you. What can I do to help?"

"Nothing, really. All we have to do is take a look around, write down what we find, and we'll be out of your way."

"All right. If I can answer any questions for you, just let me know."

The inspectors began walking around the outside of the house first. Sam went out there to watch what they did. Every so often he saw them write something on their clipboards. After walking all the way around the house, they came back inside.

One of the men seemed to be looking at the electrical wiring while the other inspected some of the water pipes. Then they both went to the second floor. There they looked in every room, especially the bathrooms. Then, they headed for the third floor. Sam raced to get up there with them.

"Will you look at this place?" one of them said.

"Why would a family need this much security equipment."

"It was here when we moved in," Sam told them. "But my dad says it'll be good for our guests."

"Guests? You mean like family and such?"

"You'll have to ask him." Then, Sam dashed back downstairs.

The men stayed up there for a very long time before they came back downstairs. One of them saw Sam. "Would you get your father for us please?"

Sam quickly brought him back to the living room.

"Most everything looks good to us. But we were really surprised to see all that video gear on the third floor."

"I know. Isn't it something?"

"What do you plan to do with it?"

"Leave it up there, I guess."

"Yeah, but what for?"

"Well, it'll provide great security for our guests."

"That's what your son said. You plan to have a lot of family come to visit?"

"Family? No," he said with a laugh. "We're turning this place into a bed and breakfast."

"You are?" they said together. Then, the men began flipping through the many pages on their clipboards.

"Doesn't say anything about a bed and breakfast on the permits."

"No. I know it doesn't. We planned to fix it up and then make the applications."

One of the men cleared his throat, and crossed his arms holding the clipboard against his chest. "Well ... this changes everything," he said, as he shook his head. "We have to go back to the office and look into the regulations. We'll be back."

"Are we in some sort of trouble?"

"Not like with the law or anything," one of the men said. "But if you want a bed and breakfast, you're gonna have to tear this place up and start over from scratch."

"What?" Sam's mother said as she came into the room.

"We'll be back," they told her. "But I wouldn't do any more work until we do."

After they left, Sam's mother buried her face in her hands and started to cry. "This is terrible ... just terrible."

His father put his arms around her and said, "I don't see how it could get much worse."

Sam clenched his fists. He'd do just about anything to keep his mother from crying.

CHAPTER 15

Sam invited his cousin to spend the night. Shelly came over too. She decided to sleep up in the dollhouse room, but Sam and Scooter wanted to sleep in the big living room.

Just before dark, Spooky started to act nervous, whimpered and let out a low growl. Sam heard the dog barking sounds from outside. When he looked out, he saw a car coming up the drive.

"Dad. Mom," he called out. "You'd better come in here."

By the time his parents came into the room, someone knocked at the door. His father opened it. There stood those same two police officers from before.

"Good evening," the taller one said. "We wanted to stop by and let you know the four men we caught are out of jail."

"They broke out?" Scooter asked with a quiver in his voice.

The other officer smiled. "I think you've been watching a little too much TV."

"Well, what then?" Sam's father asked.

"Didn't have enough evidence to hold them."

"Not enough evidence?" Sam demanded. "What about the tons of papers and pictures up there where they were hiding."

"There might have been papers, but by the time we made our investigation, all we found were those pictures."

"That's impossible." Sam's eyes darted over toward Scooter who squirmed and looked a little uncomfortable. "What about the shoes?" Sam continued.

"What about them?"

"Well, you found four guys with no shoes and we had four pairs of shoes upstairs with no guys."

Both officers laughed. "It isn't a crime to walk around with no shoes, son. Shoot, if it was, half the boys in Louisiana would be in jail."

"But the papers. They had notes about who those guys were."

"I'm sorry, but we didn't see any papers. Unless you can come up with them and prove any of this, I'm afraid it's out of our hands. And besides, after the scare you gave them, I doubt they'd ever be stupid enough to come anywhere near here again."

"Anyway," the other officer said, "we thought you'd like to know. And since you don't have a regular phone out here yet, we decided to run out and tell you." He looked around the room and added, "I must say, you've really turned this place around."

"Thank you," Sam's mother said. "But we have a long way to go."

The police smiled and left the house. Sam watched again as they drove away. Just the idea those four scary men could be out there in the dark someplace made him shiver.

Later that night, after everyone had gone to bed, Sam asked his cousin, "What do you think could have happened to the papers?"

"Search me. I didn't take 'em."

Sam rose up on one elbow. "I never said you did."

"Well … in case you were going to … I … I … um. I didn't take them … all right?"

"Don't get so touchy. You'd think you were one of those other guys."

"Forget it. Let's just get to sleep."

That took Sam a long time. There was no way he would be

able to switch off all the images in his brain. He thought about the first time he ever saw the mansion and how it had frightened him. He remembered coming back in the dark and how much worse that was until they scared the men away. When he heard them fall down the stairs again in his mind, it made him smile. Finally, he went to sleep.

Then at around midnight, Sam heard something on the front porch. He shook his cousin. "Scooter. You awake?"

"I am now."

"I heard something."

"Where?"

"Out on the porch."

"Cut it out. You're just trying to scare me." Then his voice went higher. "And it's working."

"No, really. I heard it. Somebody's out there."

Darkness enveloped the living room. Not one light had been left on in the whole house. Sam noticed there wasn't any light coming from the moon either. And his parents were all the way upstairs someplace.

"What should we do?" Scooter asked.

But, before Sam could say a word, a strange shrill howling came from the other side of the front door. That was followed by a scratching sound.

"Those guys are back and they're trying to get in," Scooter warned.

The boys crawled like commandoes on their hands and knees to the staircase. Once there, they bolted all the way to the top, skidded around the corner and blasted through the door to Sam's parents' room.

"Dad! Mom! Wake up! Somebody's trying to get in the house."

"Wha … who … huh?" his father asked in a groggy fog.

"What's happening?" his mother added with a yawn.

"Downstairs. Hurry."

By this time, Shelly was awakened by all the commotion. She came screaming into the room and hid under the covers of the big bed.

"Get your baseball bat," Sam's father told him.

Sam darted to his room and brought two of them. He gave a metal bat to his dad and kept the wooden one for himself. In slow motion, they started back down the stairs toward the front door. The howling continued and so did the scratching sound. Just as they came to the door, all the sounds stopped.

"What do you think?" Sam whispered.

"Scooter. You open the door when I tell you. Sam and I will stand on each side. When the door swings open, you duck and we'll knock the stuffin's out of whoever is on the other side." Sam smiled when he heard that.

Scooter reached for the doorknob. As he did, the other two raised the bats above their heads.

"Ready? Now!"

The door flung open and Scooter ducked, but before anyone could make another move, something darted past them and ran into the living room. Sam's father switched on the lights and all three turned toward the room. Sam also saw his mother and Shelly huddled together at the top of the stairs.

"What was that?" Scooter asked.

That's when a little head popped up. "Spooky!" Sam called out. "That was you?"

His father took a deep breath. "From now on, let's make sure the little guy is in for the night when we go to bed. Okay?"

"Okay," Sam said as he scooped the small dog into his arms. "I forgot about him this time." Even after everyone had gone back to bed, and Spooky was safely tucked in under Sam's arm for the night, Sam didn't get much sleep. He kept thinking about those men and where they might be right now.

In the morning, his mother made a big breakfast in their beautiful, new kitchen. Sam thought they were going to have just another day of work in the old house when his father said, "We're planning something a little different for today. Scooter and Shelly are invited too."

"Invited to what?" Scooter asked.

"A pirate adventure."

Shelly shrieked.

Scooter stood up. "You mean one of those cruises?"

"That's exactly what I mean."

"I've always wanted to do that, only my family never had the time."

"We're taking one today. And the train is leaving in five minutes."

Shelly's eyes darted around the room. "Train? What train?"

Sam laughed. "It's just something my dad likes to say to get us all moving on time."

The children hurried to get the things they needed. Then, it was off to the harbor. When they parked the car, Sam saw a big wooden ship with tall sails, waiting at the dock. "Is that *our* boat, Dad?"

"It certainly is."

"I'm so excited," Shelly said as she hugged herself.

Sam's mother smiled. "You've all worked so hard in the house. We wanted to reward you and to get away from all of that for a day."

They were met at the dock by a crusty-looking sea captain. Only he was dressed like a pirate with his pirate hat, a patch over one eye, and Sam thought he might have a wooden leg. He reminded Sam of Captain Jack a little.

The captain walked onto the ship and over to where a bright, green parrot sat on a wooden perch. "And this is my first mate."

"Does he have a name?" Scooter asked.

"That he does, boy, that he does. I call him iTunes."

"iTunes? Why iTunes?"

The captain thundered with a hearty laugh. "Because he

knows so many songs."

No sooner had he said that than the parrot began bobbing up and down. Then he clearly sang out, "Fifteen men on a dead man's chest."

The other crew members standing nearby sang back, "Yo-ho-ho and a bottle of rum!"

All of the sailors on the ship were dressed as pirates. When the family turned and looked, they noticed that several other people were already walking around, looking at all the ropes, anchors, and cannon.

"Do we get to eat on the ship, too?" Sam asked.

"Only if you're bad," the captain told him.

"Bad? Why bad?"

"Because this is a pirate ship. Ever hear about a good pirate?"

Now Scooter laughed. "I think I'm gonna like this trip. These are *my* kind of pirates."

"That's right, mates. And by the time we get back, you'll all be pirates."

CHAPTER 16

Once their ship had reached choppy waters, the captain began telling stories … lots of stories. He said that many years ago, pirates sailed up and down the coast, stealing from the ships they'd catch. He told them the pirates liked to sail into the area because it had calm waters, was protected by the outer islands and had a large port.

"How do they know for sure?" a man asked.

"From some of the things they've brought back to the surface."

"Why were there so many pirates?" a girl asked.

"Because ports like ours had ships coming in and out with lots of valuable cargo on board."

"But what about the pirates?" another boy asked.

"Ah, yes, the pirates. We have all these rivers where small boats could come in at night. Those pirates would hide their loot and be gone again, before the sun came up, without anyone seeing them."

"Hide it? Where?" Sam asked.

"Why, buried it in the ground. What else? They say some even went way up river"

"But where?"

The captain held his belly, let out a thunderous laugh again and slapped his knee. "If I knew that, would I be out here sailing around with tour groups?"

Sam smiled and winked at Scooter.

"What can you tell us about Lafitte?" a man asked.

The captain stroked his beard. "Well, sir, some people called him a pirate, and others thought of him as a hero." He looked out over the water and squinted his eyes. "Some think he still sails these waters." Then he leaned forward and looked directly at Sam, who felt that familiar chill go up his back. "He had a lot to do with our winning the Battle of New Orleans," the captain continued. "And he and his brother worked as blacksmiths. But later, people called him the Pirate King. Why, at one time, he had a thousand people working for him."

Several people whistled.

"Much of his life and death are still a mystery. But there were many other pirates who plundered ships in those days."

Then the captain said the oddest thing. "Folks say the treasures were buried in the dirt all over south Louisiana, and they're covered with human skulls and cross bones."

That made Sam shiver.

"Others say some of it's still out there ... just waitin' for someone to come along and dig it up." Then he bellowed with laughter once more.

Sam enjoyed eating out on the ocean. Seagulls flew along behind the ship, watching for any scrap of food that might land in the water. When the ship came back to port, Sam noticed how calm the water was after they passed the outer islands. It made sense how pirates would use those same waters to come in with their smaller boats. He remembered the river wasn't far from their mansion.

Could it be?

Scooter and Shelly had permission to spend the night again when they returned from their voyage. But late in the afternoon, Sam's parents had to go into town.

"We shouldn't be long," his mother told them. "But if it starts to get dark, just put a few lights on. I've left a pizza in the freezer for you. You can heat it up and wait for us to come home."

"I wish we had a phone here so you could call us," Sam said.

"Do you have yours, Scooter?" Sam's dad asked.

"No, sir. Daddy borrowed it. This time *his* battery was dead."

"You'll be all right. And Spooky is here to help keep you safe."

Sam looked down at his little dog. "I'd rather take my chances by myself," he said. Spooky whined and cocked his head to one side.

After his parents drove away, Shelly ran right back up to the dollhouse room. Sam and Scooter dashed to the third floor to play with the video equipment.

"I still can't figure out who took those papers," Sam said.

Scooter kept quiet for a minute or so. Then he said, "I took some stuff over to my house."

Sam raised his eyebrows. "What kind of stuff?"

"Papers and junk."

"You did? Why?"

"I don't know. I thought it'd be cool to have something that belonged to a bunch of real crooks."

"But because you did that, they got away again."

Scooter looked down. "I know."

"What did you do with that stuff?"

"Crammed it under my bed."

"We need to get it back."

He looked up to Sam again. "Right now?"

"No. We aren't supposed to leave till my parents get home. But after that, we need to give it to the police in case they ever catch those guys again."

"I guess so."

"You guess so? What you did was almost as bad as what they were doing up here."

A couple hours later, the sun went down, and it began getting dark outside. Sam probably wouldn't have noticed except his stomach started growling at about the same time. "Let's go make that pizza," he said.

"Race you to the kitchen," his cousin yelled as he sprinted halfway to the door. The boys came to the kitchen at almost the same time. When Shelly heard them running and yelling, she hurried down, too.

"How could you guys be hungry again?" she asked.

"Who needs a reason," her brother said. "We just are."

She put her hands on her stomach. "But I'm still stuffed from the boat ride."

Before long, the delightful smell of pepperoni pizza filled the kitchen. Sam glanced at his watch. Then he looked outside. "I sure hope they get back soon."

The children sat at a round, wooden kitchen table so they could eat and talk.

"What did you like best about the pirate ship?" Shelly asked as she picked at her piece of pepperoni pizza.

"I liked the black pirate flag with the skull on it," Scooter told them proudly.

"My favorites were the clothes all the pirate sailors had on," Shelly said.

"What is it with girls and clothes?" Scooter asked in a disgusted tone.

"Well, they were cute, that's all."

"The pirates or their clothes?" he mocked.

"I liked the stories the captain told," Sam added. "I mean, thinking about pirates out there on the same water as we were."

Scooter laughed. "Or under it."

"But just think about the treasure that could be buried around this whole area."

"Aw, people probably found all of it by now."

"Then how come everybody's so excited over finding sunken

ships?" Sam asked, "And what about your map?"

"It's just a legend. You said yourself my map and the treasure probably aren't real."

"Yes, it is. And we heard that a bunch of cannon have been brought back to shore in the last several years."

"You didn't hear that," Scooter said.

"Yes, I did," Sam told him. "We took a tour one night and they told us all about it. But they told a bunch of ghost stories, too."

Scooter rubbed his hands together. "Now we're gettin' someplace."

In the distance, Sam heard the sounds of dogs barking. But this time, he thought nothing of it.

A few minutes later, without warning, every light in the house went out.

"Oh, this is just great," he complained. "Does the power go out like that all the time around here?"

"Only during bad storms," his cousin told him.

"Are you sure?"

"I'm absolutely ..." only he didn't finish. That's because they heard a thump on the front porch, which was followed by the sounds of chains dragging across the boards out there. Only that was nothing compared to the howling that followed.

"Would you please go out there and get your dog?" Scooter whispered. "See what he dragged up on the porch this time."

In a trembling voice, Sam said, "He's right next to me now, shaking harder than I am."

"You mean that's *not* Spooky out there?"

"Oh, it's spooky all right, just not my dog."

Shelly started crying softly.

"Your parents then," Scooter asked.

Sam shook his head. "They would *never* try to scare us like this. I'm sure of it."

"You don't think ... ghosts?"

That made Shelly scream and stomp her foot.

"Cut it out, Scooter, you're scaring your sister." Sam demanded.

Then, from outside, a low menacing voice said, "Why are you in my house?"

None of the children said a word.

"Get ... out ... of ... my ... house!" the voice threatened.

Sam wanted to run to the third floor and look on the video monitor from the front door camera, so he could find out who or what was out there. But he couldn't do that since the power had been cut. He eased himself nearer to the front of the house. That's when he looked out and saw four shadows on a sheer white curtain in the living room.

"It's them," he whispered.

"Them who?" Scooter asked.

"Them!"

"Oh, no."

Sam turned to his cousin. "Why don't you start talking to those guys. I've got a plan."

Scooter's voice quivered. "I've got a better idea. Why don't *you* talk to them?"

"And then what?"

"Then I won't have to."

"Do what I told you. I'm going out there."

"No, Sam. No!" Shelly cried.

CHAPTER 17

Sam grabbed a flashlight from a kitchen drawer and an old sheet off the laundry pile. Then, he slipped silently out the back door and into the darkness. When he reached the side of the house, he stopped at the double doors covering a large opening into the cellar.

He and his father had gone down into the cellar a few days earlier to see if anything interesting might still be stored down there. His father had told him, "Always make sure these doors are closed."

Without making a sound, Sam leaned down, opened the first door and slowly laid it flat on the ground, uncovering half of the hole. Then he moved over, opened the second door and set it on the ground, too. Carefully, he walked around the open cellar and continued toward the front porch.

He heard his cousin inside the house. "Who are you guys? What do you want?"

"We want you out of our house."

"But it isn't *your* house. These other people bought it. They own the mansion now."

"We'll see about that," one of the men said. "The place is haunted. After we … I mean the ghosts that live here get through with them, your friends won't want nothin' to do with this place."

"What ghosts?" Scooter asked. "Y'all were the ones making all that racket. We saw your stuff upstairs."

"You did ... I mean ... no you didn't. It ain't our stuff."

"Shut up, you idiot," another ordered.

"Sorry, boss. I wasn't tinkin.'"

"That's your problem. You're never *tinkin,*' just talkin', talkin', talkin'. All the time talkin'."

"No, I don't. Some times I'm sleepin'."

"Well, right now you're awake and you're talkin'."

"Oh."

Sam turned back and walked carefully around the house until he reached all the way to the other side of the porch. His cousin kept the four men busy.

"Our parents are coming back any minute."

"Sure they are. We ain't dumb enough to fall for that one."

"What *are* you dumb enough to fall for?" Scooter asked.

"That ain't funny, kid."

Sam covered his mouth to keep from making a sound. He could hardly keep from laughing when he heard that. He knew that Scooter had no idea what he was about to try.

"When they come back," Scooter said, "we're calling the police."

"Right," the boss said. "And how do you expect to do that with no power and no phone?"

"Uh ... you guys ever heard of a *cell* phone?" Scooter said. "Funny thing about cellphones. The way I heard it, you don't get one where you're going."

"Oh, yeah? And where would that be?"

"To a *jail* cell!"

Sam watched as a short fat man said, "Dis kid is a real comedian."

"And you can be quiet, too," the boss commanded.

Sam kept watching as the boss tried to shake the door and

get it open. He heard the cousins inside run away from the door, screaming. That's when he reached down for the rake he'd been using the day before. He felt around in the dirt until his hand bumped into something. *I sure am glad there aren't any ghosts. Or I'd be running for the woods right now.*

He grabbed the long handle with one hand and slipped it under his sheet. *I hope this works.* With his other hand, he eased the flashlight under the sheet. Then, he started howling like a wolf. Just as the men turned to see where that awful sound was coming from, Sam switched on the flashlight and began making the sheet float back and forth behind the porch railing.

"Wooohhh!" Sam moaned as he continued moving the sheet around. "Wooohhh!" he went again.

One of the men yelled, "Crimeny, Boss. Maybe dis place *is* haunted."

"Let's get outta here," the boss ordered.

The men dashed to the opposite end of the porch and leaped over the railing. Sam took off running after them. He watched as they continued on around the side of the house. Then he stopped.

"Five … four … three … two … one," he counted down in his head. That's when he heard it. First, the men cried out in terror. Then they crashed together as they bumped, thumped, and crumpled down the rickety wooden steps. Sam snapped his fingers as a smile came to his face. "Another strike. I really should start bowling more."

He hurried in the direction of that tremendous racket. By the time he got there, all he heard were the moaning sounds of four men who'd taken quite a fall. He switched his light back on and pointed it toward the ground. That's when he saw all of them lying in a tangled pile at the bottom of the cellar steps.

The boss managed to raise his fist and threaten, "We're gonna get you, boy." Then they began to untangle their legs and arms. While they tried their best to do that, Sam pulled up one of the doors and slammed it shut.

"Hey, whadaya tink you're doin'?"

"I *tink* I'm about to lock you guys in there." He took another moment to look in one more time with his light. When he did, all four men started climbing back up the stairs. Sam hurried to lift the second heavy, wooden cellar door. Just as the men came close to the top of the stairs, wham! The door slammed shut. And when it did, it hit the first man, who hit the second, who hit the third until Sam heard all four collide again onto the dirt floor at the bottom of the cellar.

He took his rake handle and slipped it through two large, rusted-metal handles; one on each door. The men found their way to the top of the stairs again and began pounding and yelling.

"Let us outa here."

"Oh, when I get my hands on you …"

"No, me first."

"Shut up all of yas. We're stuck down here. Now try to find a way out."

But Sam already knew the only way out was the way they'd gone in. Just then he heard the sound of a car and saw lights coming up the driveway. He ran to meet it. The other children dashed out the front door at the same time.

"Dad! Mom! Hurry. Call the police."

His father jumped out of the car. "Wait a minute. What's going on?"

"Just call them. Hurry." Then Sam rushed back to the side of the house. He heard his mother start to dial the phone.

"What do I tell them?" she asked.

"Tell them to get out here. Right now!" Sam called back over his shoulder.

When he and his father reached the cellar doors, they could still hear the men pounding and yelling.

"Who's down there?" his father asked.

Sam shined his light on the doors. "It's those men I told you about. The ones the police let go."

"They came back here?"

"They sure did."

"How did you get them down there?"

"Remember when you told me, 'Always make sure these doors are closed?'"

"Yes."

"Well ... I ... *opened* them!"

"Sam, what a *great* idea."

He smiled. "It was, wasn't it?"

"But how? What made them go down there?"

He picked up the sheet and put his light under it. "It was a *real* ghost, Dad."

Then they began laughing together. Scooter came over and asked, "What's so funny?"

"I just told my dad a true ghost story."

"Funniest one I ever heard."

A voice called from the cellar. "Would one of youse guys be so kind as to let us outta here? A couple of us is scared of the dark, see?"

Sam saw the flashing lights of police cars turning into the lane. "Somebody'll let you guys out in *just* a minute," he told them.

"Aw, tanks a lot, kid."

Several police rushed up to where Sam and his father sat on the doors, keeping guard over the cellar. They recognized two of the officers who had been to the house before. "Who you got down there?" one of them asked.

Sam said through a wide grin, "The same guys who left their shoes upstairs."

"But, how did they ...?"

"I'll tell you later. Right now, I think you should take them back to jail where they belong."

"On what charge?" he asked Sam's father.

"How about trespassing?"

"How do you figure?"

"We aren't open yet. Only our family should be here now, except for some delivery people during the daytime."

Sam looked over to Scooter. "And my cousin has something he wants to tell you."

Scooter looked down at the ground and kicked his toe in the dirt.

"Yes, son, what is it?" the officer asked.

"I ... um ... I sorta took some stuff from the third floor before you guys first came out here."

"That's tampering with evidence at a crime scene. Did you know that?"

He shook his head, "No, sir."

"What kind of stuff?" another officer asked.

"Papers and junk."

"They tell all about who these guys are and what they did to try and keep people away," Sam said.

"Where are they now?"

"Under my bed at home."

"Murphy," the officer called out.

"Sir?"

"Take this boy home and bring me those papers right away."

"Yes, sir."

One of the other officers removed Sam's rake handle from the doors while the others brought the four men out and put them in handcuffs.

"Tanks, I was really gettin' a scared almost half ta death down there."

"You'll feel a lot safer in jail."

"I don't like that a *lot*."

"Too late. You gentlemen are going to jail ... where you belong."

"Did ya hear dat, boss? He called us gentlemens."

"Shut up, ya big baboon."

"Ohhkaay."

They were quickly led away and the police cars drove back toward the main road.

Sam's mother ran up to him. "I'm so sorry we were late. We just couldn't help it."

"It's okay, Mom."

"No, it isn't," Shelly said. "Those guys really scared me."

Sam's father put his arm around her shoulder. "Well, they're gone now. Let's get inside." Then he looked at the house. "Why are all the lights out, Sam?"

"Those guys turned them off somehow."

His father walked over to a large box on the side of the house, opened the door, pushed up on a big handle and lights came on all over inside."

Shelly looked up at the house. "I like that a lot better than the dark."

CHAPTER 18

Shelly had returned home the night before when an officer took her brother to get the papers. Just after breakfast the next morning, Scooter started pounding at the front door.

"Come on in," Sam's father called out, "it's open."

When the door swung open, Scooter said, "After last night, I thought every door would be locked."

Sam walked over to him. "Did you give them the papers?"

His cousin nodded.

"Were they mad?"

He nodded again.

"At least the police have them now."

"I know, but how did you get those guys to go down in the cellar last night?"

"I made a ghost."

"You *made* a ghost?"

"Yeah, with my flashlight and a sheet."

"How dumb. And they fell for it?"

Sam folded his arms. "Boy, did *they* ever. It's amazing what some people will believe ... if they want to."

"Yeah, amazing," Scooter said, followed by a nervous laugh.

He was about to close the front door when another car came

down the lane. "I wonder who that is?" Sam's father said.

His mother looked out. "Oh, I know, it's the inspector coming back with his report."

Sam's father took a deep breath. "I hope it's good news."

This time, only one of the men from before stepped out of the car. He had his clipboard again and a worried look on his face. He shook his head as he walked up. "Afraid I've got some very bad news."

Sam's father stepped forward. "How bad?"

"Let's take a little walk around the place. I'll show you each one."

As they walked, Sam and Scooter went with them.

"First, you have to do things totally differently if you plan to open as a bed and breakfast. If you were to live here with just your family, most of the things on my list could be crossed off."

"But we couldn't afford this place for just our little family. And it's so big. We're only three people. We don't need this much space."

"You could try and sell it to a bigger family."

"We wouldn't be interested."

"After you see my list, you might want to change your mind."

"Where should we start?"

"Let's go to the third floor first."

Up there, he pointed to the ceiling. The third floor wasn't finished or decorated like the rest of the house. A person could see right up into the roof.

"At least half your beams need to be replaced and most of the roof."

"You mean just the shingles?"

"No, sir ... the whole roof—wood and all. And there's a lot of exposed, outdated wiring up here. The place could burn down."

"You're talking a lot of money."

The man nodded. "I know, but this is one of the easiest floors."

"What do you mean?"

He led them back down to the second floor where he pointed out other wiring and plumbing that had to be replaced. "And the bathrooms are too small. You'll need bigger doors, and they all have to be accessible for people with disabilities. Then, you need fire escapes, a sprinkler system, an elevator, and ramps everywhere. I've made out a detailed list of everything."

"How's a person expected to pay for all these things?"

"That's why not too many people like yourselves try to take on an old dum ... I mean a place like this."

"All right, what else?"

"Well, that brings us to the two biggest problems you got."

"What could be bigger than you've already shown me?"

He motioned for them to follow him out the front door. As they stood on the porch he said, "If you expect paying guests to come here, you have to put in a paved road. Now it can be concrete, brick, blacktop ... we don't care. It just can't be dirt and gravel like it is now. But your biggest problem is the sewer."

"Sewer?"

"See, this old house still has a septic system."

"What's that?" Sam asked.

"Think of it as a big tank in the ground. With all the people you plan to have out here, laundry, and that sorta stuff, you gotta hook up to the main sewer line."

"How far away is that?" Sam's father asked.

The man pointed all the way to a paved road a long distance away. "It runs by that building over there."

Sam's father shook his head. "This is impossible."

"What's impossible?" Sam's mother asked as she walked onto the porch.

"Wait till you see the list they've made for us. It's going to cost a fortune."

The inspector handed the list to Sam's father, tipped his hat and turned to leave. Then he stopped and turned back. He laughed slightly and said, "You know what they say about this place."

"That only an idiot would ever buy it?"

"No, sir. What they say is, 'he who owns the mansion, owns the treasure.'"

Sam's father clenched his fists and fumed, "If I hear those words one more time."

Then, the inspector laughed again. "Yeah, some treasure. Look, you seem like nice people. I'm sorry. I really am." But as he walked toward his car he shook his head and muttered again, "He who owns the mansion."

"What are we going to do now?" Sam's mother cried.

"I'll just have to go to the bank again, explain our situation and show him the list. He's got to lend us more money."

Later that day, he returned from the bank. Sam noticed a sad look on his father's face. He shuffled inside to talk with Sam's mother. They were still talking when Scooter headed home and Sam went in for supper. He heard his mother softly crying in the living room. Sam walked over and put his hand on her shoulder. "It'll be okay, Mom. I know it will … somehow."

She only smiled through her red, teary eyes.

"What did the bank say, Dad?"

"They'll see what they can do. But the man made no promises."

"What then?"

"He said we can have enough money to do some of the things. But I just have to keep going or we'll never be able to open."

"What's first?"

"While I was in town, I talked with an excavator."

"What do they do?"

"They dig a lot of holes in the ground."

Sam laughed. "They must have been the ones who messed up our backyard."

"Well, these men come in with all sorts of digging equipment. Then they lay big pipes in the ground to hook us up to the main sewer like the inspector said."

"When are they coming?"

"Tomorrow morning."

"But?" his mother said.

"Look, all our lives we wanted to set up a place like this so we can show love and hope to other people. You never know how that might help them."

"I know, but what if our plans are just *our* plans?"

He took a deep breath. "You know how long we've thought about this. I don't think it was a mistake, and I don't believe we did it only on our own, do you?"

She shook her head and wiped her eyes.

"Then we'll just have to keep moving forward. No matter how impossible it might look right now."

I sure hope this works out. Sam hugged his mom.

CHAPTER 19

The next day, Sam and his family worked around the house like they had been doing for weeks. Sam began to wonder if it was worth it. As he dragged a few things outside to the trash pile in the back, he heard a loud noise. He ran to the frontyard in time to see several big trucks rumbling up the lane. A cloud of dust billowed all around them until they reached the circle in the front yard.

This is a bigger job than I thought. No wonder it costs so much.

It wasn't long before workmen began digging a deep trench into the dirt with their heavy equipment. After a while, Sam became bored with it all, just watching them, and he started back to work. That's when Scooter and Shelly came over.

"Those guys are really tearing up your front yard," Scooter said.

"And our life, too."

The boys worked together bringing wallpaper scraps, dry paint cans, and carpet pieces outside to take to the dump. At lunchtime, the men weren't even half way finished digging their trench. The cousins made sandwiches in the kitchen. Shelly stayed inside to eat, and the boys walked back out on the front porch so they could watch the work.

"Do you think the papers I gave the cops will keep those guys in jail now?"

"I hope so."

"Me, too. I don't ever want to see them again."

Sam laughed. "I still can't believe I scared four grown men with a silly little pretend ghost."

"I wanted to talk with you about that."

"My ghost? What about it?"

Scooter shook his head. "I mean all ghosts. I really have terrible bad dreams sometimes. Do you think that's because ..."

"Because you don't go to church and stuff?"

Scooter nodded.

"It's more than that. But you should start coming with us anyway. Your Mom and Dad and Shelly too."

"I think we'd like that. My parents have been talking about your parents."

Sam smiled. "That sounds dangerous."

"They couldn't figure out how come y'all are still working on this place."

"You know the reason," Sam said.

"I know. You told me once that it's because y'all want to give other people hope. I thought, if it's that important for strangers ... then why not family."

Sam smiled again.

"We kind of decided we'd like to go to church with you and see what it's all about."

"Great. Let's go tell my parents."

The boys jumped up and ran into the house.

By the end of the day, one of the workers came to the door. "Mr. Cooper, would it be okay if we left our trucks out here tonight? We'll be back again early in the morning."

"It's fine with us if you don't block the lane."

"We won't, and I made sure all the pipe is out of the way too."

"Fine."

"We finished our digging. Tomorrow, we'll start laying the pipeline."

Scooter and Shelly had permission to stay over again. The children played in the game room when Sam heard the dogs barking again. "Uh-oh," he said. Then he rushed up stairs to the third floor. The other children followed him.

When they ran in, Sam turned a switch and the dog stopped barking.

"Ah, that's how it works," Scooter said. "I wondered why I never saw any dumb dogs around here."

Spooky growled when he heard that.

"Not you, Spooky."

Sam pointed to one of the monitors. "See, a motion sensor set off the dog bark. And that tipped off the guys up here when we came out the first time. All they had to do was get ready to scare anyone who got near the place."

"But when we snuck up from the backyard?"

"There weren't any sensors back there, so they never expected that."

"They were pretty dumb, huh?"

"*Really* dumb. They actually thought I was a real ghost."

"I loved that part," Shelly said with a giggle.

Her brother smiled along with a nervous laugh.

"Look at camera number six." Sam pointed to the monitor, and the children watched a police car turning into the circle drive. They hurried downstairs to find out what was wrong now.

When they reached the main floor, Sam's father had just opened the door.

"Sorry to bother you folks again, but you don't have a phone yet, and I didn't get your cell number."

"What *cell* number did those other guys get?" Scooter asked.

"That's a good one. I'll have to tell the guys back at the department. But I thought you'd like to know the papers you boys found, along with the pictures, gave us all the evidence we needed."

Both boys beamed.

"The judge says we have a pretty strong case against them. Those men won't get the chance to bother you ever again."

"That's a relief," Sam's father said.

"Y'all have a good night now."

"We will … and thanks."

"You can thank those boys. They're the ones who ran them off before they could destroy the evidence."

Sam and Scooter just stood there and grinned.

Sam's father looked back at him and shook his finger. "You're still in trouble about all that."

They'd all had a very long day. The family and cousins decided it was time for bed. On this night, the boys stayed up in Sam's ship room.

After the lights were off, Scooter said, "Ever think what it'd be like to sail on a big ship, all over the world?"

"Sometimes. But I kinda like it around here now."

"That's just because you're new. I've been here for *ever*."

"Twelve years is hardly forever," Sam said.

"It is when you're only twelve."

"Remember when we went out for that sailing cruse not long ago?" Sam asked.

"You mean the pirate ship trip?"

"Uh-huh. It really got me thinking. And I'd like to work someplace where I could study the ocean."

"Who studies the ocean?" Scooter asked.

"Not just the water. People learn about fish and sea life. There are all kinds of plants and shipwrecks, too."

"That's what I want to do," Scooter said.

"What?"

"Be a treasure hunter. Divers have found lots of neat stuff down there."

"Yeah," Sam said. "Maybe I could do something like that to help my parents pay for this place."

"Be serious. They don't hire too many kids to go deep-sea diving."

Sam laughed. "No, guess not. And my friend Captain Jack might have something to say about not going treasure hunting."

"Who's Captain Jack?"

"He's a good friend back in Harper's Inlet. You'd like him."

Later that night, a tremendous thunderstorm awakened Sam. He found Spooky already hiding under one of the pillows, and the little dog shook all over. Sam reached over and patted him on his back. That seemed to help. Spooky pulled his head out and put his cold, wet nose on Sam's cheek. Then he started licking all over his head.

"Quit it, Spooky."

His cousin never woke up. Sam figured Scooter had probably lived through worse storms than this before, but he stayed awake until it stopped raining. When he woke up the next morning, his cousin had already gone downstairs. Sam dragged himself down to the kitchen where his mother fixed him some toast and juice. Then, he ran out looking for Scooter. He found him pulling weeds in the garden and picking up sticks from the storm.

When he saw Sam, Scooter said, "I never knew it rained last night. Did you hear it?"

"Heard it *and* saw it."

"A big one, huh?"

"Sure was. I couldn't believe you slept through the whole thing."

They worked together until the excavators returned. The boys hurried around front to listen.

"You must have gotten more rain up here than we did in town. Most of your trench is washed out."

"What now?" Sam's father asked.

"Gotta start all over again."

127

Sam's father took in an extra deep breath. "It's just one thing after another around here. Sometimes even I wonder if ..." Then, he looked at Sam.

The man asked, "Wonder what?"

"Never mind. You men better get started."

Sam and Scooter went around the back again where they picked out a shovel.

"What's the job this time," Scooter asked.

"My mom wants a couple bird feeders on posts so the guests can see them while they eat in the dining room."

"Do you know how to do that?"

"Dig a hole?" Sam laughed.

"No. I mean put in a bird feeder."

"All we have to do is dig the holes. My dad'll take it from there."

The ground was softer now because of the rain. It didn't take any time at all before the boys began on the second hole.

"Wouldn't that be something," Scooter said.

"Wouldn't what be something?"

"If after all this time and those goons who were upstairs with all their equipment, we were the ones to dig up the treasure."

"I'm thinking that's just a story," Sam said in disgust. "Now keep digging."

They started digging the second hole but didn't find anything besides roots and rocks at first. Then, something happened. Sam's shovel struck something hard in the dirt.

"I think I found something," he said to Scooter.

Both boys dropped to their knees on both sides of the hole and peered in. Sam reached down and scooped dirt out of the hole and threw it to one side.

"Dad! Dad!" Sam screamed.

In seconds, his father rushed around to where the boys were. "What is it?"

"There's something down here!!"

Quickly his father joined them on the ground and helped Sam scoop out more dirt. "I feel something," he said with excitement.

Just then, Sam's mother hurried outside. Full of excitement she asked, "What is it?"

Sam's eyes were as wide open as any two eyes can get, and Scooter's were too. Neither one could say a word.

Sam's dad grunted as he struggled with something in the hole. "It could be the answer to all our problems." Then he grunted again as he tried to pull on something. "Give me that shovel again, Sam."

Sam handed him the shovel and listened as its blade scraped across a large, solid object. And that turned out to be the problem. It was large, and it was solid, because what they found was only a great big rock. Sam's mother turned and walked slowly back toward the house. His father stood up, jammed the shovel in the dirt, and turned to leave.

"Sorry, Dad," Sam nearly whispered.

His father brushed dirt from his pants. "That's okay. It's not your fault."

It was all Sam could do to stop from crying. "But I hoped … I mean … we needed it so bad."

His father nodded, "Better get back to work." He patted Sam on the shoulder, and walked away.

The boys had to start a new hole that didn't have a big rock in it. They were about to go in for lunch when they heard several blasts from loud horns on some of the trucks. They raced to the front as Sam's parents hurried out the door. Two of the men came running up to the house as fast as they could, waving their arms and yelling.

One of them called out, "You gotta come with us!"

"What now?" Sam's father asked.

"If it's going to cost us more money, we don't even want to see it or hear about it," Sam's mother added.

They all hurried out to where the other workers were standing by their trucks. One of the men jumped into the trench. The man in charge of the crew said, "We were planning to come out here this morning, lay the pipe and cover it over. But then it rained last night."

Sam's father sighed. "Yeah, we know all about what the rain did."

"You don't know everything it did."

"How much?" Sam's mother asked.

"We don't know yet."

"You mean you don't know how much it's going to cost us?"

"Cost *you*? No. I don't know how much it's going to be *worth*."

"What are we talking about here?"

They all moved closer toward the trench. The man who'd already climbed down there looked up. "It's the strangest thing I've ever seen in all the years I've been digging in this county. I mean, I've heard stories and all."

Sam's father folded his arms. "Just what is it you're getting at?"

"I've found two already."

"Found? Found two of what?"

"Well, sir, we went ahead and knocked the lock off one of them. Hank, over there, wanted to make sure they didn't have skeletons in there or anything."

"And?"

The man down in the trench pulled open the top of one of the old chests. Finally, everyone moved right up to the edge. When Sam looked down, his eyes widened. He pointed a shaking finger and said, "Dad, look!"

The first chest nearly overflowed with colorfully sparkling jewels and gold coins. When they opened the second chest, it contained silver, plates, goblets, and fine jewelry.

The local authorities were called. They rushed out to the mansion and took the chests for safekeeping. Sam's father was given a document that stated, "Although a treasure be not the number of things which are lost or abandoned or which never belonged to anybody, yet he who finds it on his own land, or on land belonging to nobody, acquires the entire ownership of it."

A man from the government told Sam's father, "At least a thousand treasure sites have been rumored in Louisiana." A big smile spread across his face. "Looks like there are only nine hundred ninety-nine left for treasure hunters now."

After a full inventory, the Cooper family received a check for far more than enough money to make all the needed repairs and to turn the old mansion into a bed and breakfast as they had always dreamed. And there was plenty more money left over ... plenty! They even gave some to each of the men on the excavation crew.

One evening several days later, Sam's father stood on the front porch, watching an orange sunset. Sam joined him.

"Beautiful sight, isn't it Sam?"

"Sure is."

"I heard it might storm tonight."

Sam's eyes scanned the entire front yard. *I wonder how many more chests are out there?* Then he whispered, "He who owns the mansion ..."

THE END

About the Author

Max Elliot Anderson—Using his extensive experience in dramatic film, video, and television commercial production, Max Elliot Anderson brings that same visual excitement and heart-pounding action to his many adventures and mysteries for middle-grade readers eight and up. Books for Boys Blog: http://booksandboysblogspot.com

71177297R00075

Made in the USA
Middletown, DE
20 April 2018